Lilliana Jones and the Temple of Groom

Rich Amooi

Lilliana Jones and the Temple of Groom

Copyright 2016 © Rich Amooi

http://www.richamooi.com

Editing by Mary Yakovets

To receive updates on new releases, exclusive deals, and occasional silly stuff, sign up for Rich's newsletter at: http://www.richamooi.com/newsletter

To my sister Amy Messerschmidt,
the most generous person I know.

Chapter One

"I would rather have laser hair removal on my upper lip for six hours without numbing cream than have lunch with you today," Lilliana Jones said into the phone. "You know the routine. If we didn't plan it, I will ban it."

Sometimes Lilly had to show her best friend tough love, since Colette was always up to something. Up to *no good* would be more accurate.

"Wait just one minute," Colette said in her typical dramatic fashion. "Who said yes when you wanted a marathon partner for the Alzheimer's fundraiser?"

"You did."

"And who got up at six in the morning to volunteer with you for that coastal clean-up day on the beach?"

Lilly sighed, knowing Colette wasn't finished yet. "You."

"And who helped you sell all those Girl Scout cookies?"

"Oh, come on. That was over twenty years ago."

"Still counts."

"I'm not meeting you for lunch."

"*I* would do it for *you*." Colette put just enough emphasis on the *I* and *You* to plant another seed in Lilly's guilt trip garden.

"Hold on." Lilly set the phone down on her desk and closed her office door. As Vice President of HR, she had an open door policy. She wanted employees at the high-tech company to always feel welcome if they ever needed to talk or had an issue with something. But conversations with Colette were on the animated side and Lilly didn't need everyone in the office to listen to her explain why she didn't want to go out to lunch today.

Lilly didn't do spontaneous.

She'd eliminated the word from her vocabulary and the corresponding act three years ago when spontaneity sent her boyfriend on a trip to Africa to find himself.

He never returned. Just like her father had done when she was a little girl.

Since the day her soul-searching douche bag of an ex decided there were more important things in life than Lilly everything had to be scheduled in advance. And there was no straying from the plan. Ever. She was certain Colette would still try to convince her to be spontaneous.

Lilly circled back around her desk and grabbed the phone. "Okay, what's so important?"

"I can't say over the phone."

Lilly waited for something more but heard nothing. "Colette. It's slice and dice day. I need to turn a department of twenty-five people into a department of ten and we have a board meeting this afternoon. Plus I have an employee who claims he missed a week of work because he got salmonella from the fried pork rinds in our vending machine."

"I need to see you in person. This can't wait. It's a matter of…"

"Life and death? Don't even… I swear I feel a monstrous migraine coming on."

"Meet me at Panda Express on Meridian and I'll explain everything."

"You're going to tell me about a life and death situation over Chinese?"

"That food takes me to my happy place."

Lilly paced back and forth in her office, going over her options. She didn't have many. If she didn't meet Colette, she'd feel guilty. She couldn't turn her back on her best friend when she was in need. If she *was* in need. Colette sounded sincere but then again, she was an accomplished actress, having toured with several theater productions, including two months performing in *Romeo and Juliet* with Orlando Bloom.

"Lilly? Please…"

"I'll be right there. And if this is another trick to get me to do something spontaneous, you're the one who'll be having laser without numbing cream."

Lilly felt she was being set up but she couldn't take a chance.

Eight minutes later she parked her sensible and practical Toyota Corolla in front of the Panda Express. Normally she would find a spot in the farthest area of the shopping center to avoid the possibility of door dings and other disasters.

Today she had no time to spare. At least she wasn't struck by lightning or sideswiped by a city bus because of her sudden change of plans.

"Thank you," she said to herself, full of gratitude.

She swung the front door to Panda Express open and walked to the back where Colette sat with two meals and two glasses of water. Not a surprise since Lilly had the same thing every time they ate there.

Colette stood and hugged Lilly, then pointed to the platter across from her. "I got you your favorite."

Lilly eyed the fried rice and double order of shrimp then brought her attention back to Colette. "You don't look distraught. I swear—"

"Sit down and eat."

She placed her purse on the open chair next to her. "Colette, if you—"

"Eat!"

Lilly pulled the chair out and sat. "You're pushy."

Colette smirked. "You still love me."

"For now…" Lilly pulled out a small bottle of hand sanitizer from her purse. "You want some?"

Colette shook her head. "No, but let me see your keychain for a second."

"Why?"

"I think I'll get my mom one for her birthday. I forgot where you got it…"

Lilly handed Colette her brass elephant key chain. "I

bought it online on Etsy."

Colette analyzed the key chain. "Oh, that's right."

Lilly squeezed hand sanitizer into her palms and rubbed her hands together until the liquid disappeared. Then she stuck the bottle back in her purse and took her first bite. She took a few more bites, wondering how long it would be before her best friend spoke.

Colette took a bite of her chicken and moaned. "Oh God." She closed her eyes and chewed slowly. "Ohhhhhhh God."

"You sound like Meg Ryan. Knock it off."

Colette swallowed and waved to someone over Lilly's shoulder. "She's here. She can be a little rough around the edges but she means well, so just go with it."

"Who?"

"Madam Love." Colette said the name as if Lilly knew who Madam Love was. As if Lilly would be fine with an unexpected lunch guest. As if Lilly had no clue her best friend was up to no good.

Lilly twisted her body around to follow Colette's gaze. A tall, slender woman entered the restaurant wearing a carrot-colored cape and a brown bandana. She looked like the world's tallest pumpkin. The woman's jewelry jingled and jangled with each step, easily heard over the noise of the customers and cooks.

Lilly swung back around. "What's going on?"

Colette bit her lower lip. "This is an intervention."

Lilly's heart rate sped up. This wasn't happening. It wasn't part of the plan and the only thing she wanted to do now was figure out the best way to kill her best friend.

Colette stood and smiled. "Madam Love. So glad you could join us."

"Darling." Madam Love air-kissed Colette and turned to Lilly. "You must be—"

"Out of here." Lilly stood and grabbed her purse.

Colette taunted Lilly with her keys. "Good luck with that."

Lilly lunged for the keys but she wasn't fast enough to grab them. "God! I can't believe I fell for that. Your mom's birthday isn't for another six months."

"She celebrates bi-annually now."

"Right. It was bad enough you changed my plans for lunch but then you invited a psychic?"

"Psychic is so last century," Madam Love said. "I'm The Human Whisperer. Anyway, I already know so much about you from watching you."

"I can't believe you did this, Colette. You lied. You told me this was a matter of life and death."

"It is." Colette squeezed Lilly's arm and frowned. "Yours."

Lilly laughed, but it came out more like a cackle. "I'm not dying."

"Actually, you are." Madam Love pulled out a chair and sat, making herself right at home. "I felt the vibration as I approached your table. You're dying on the *inside*. I'm certain of it."

Ridiculous.

Dying on the inside? This woman didn't even know her. Sure, Lilly's life was safe, maybe even as plain as her morning bagel, but was that a bad thing?

"Just sit and we'll talk over lunch," Colette said, putting her arm around Madam Love. "She's amazing. I never told you about her because I knew you didn't believe in psychics but she predicted I would meet the love of my life in a park. I met Simon a week later."

"You went to the park, found the first thing with testicles and hit on him. Just a coincidence... Look at you." Lilly gestured to Colette's long blonde hair and slim body. "You're the most beautiful woman I know."

"No. You are." Colette placed both hands on Lilly's shoulders and pushed down. "Sit. The intervention starts now."

Madam Love reached over and grabbed the fortune cookie from Lilly's tray. Then she took Colette's. "These can be distractions and must be eliminated." Madam Love ate both cookies and laughed at each of the fortunes, not bothering to share them with Colette and Lilly.

Lilly didn't like that she was taking her time. "Since I'm a prisoner here can we get going with this?"

Maybe Madam Love got paid by the hour. Finally, it looked like she was ready. She opened her purse and stuck her nose inside.

Lilly couldn't believe this was happening. "Don't tell me... Tarot cards? A crystal ball? Maybe an Ouija board?"

"Do I look old school to you?" Madam Love gestured to her cape proudly. She pulled out a glass pyramid from her purse and placed it in the middle of the table. It couldn't have been over three inches tall, filled with tiny transparent purple stones and what appeared to be metal shavings.

Lilly tilted her head to the side. "What is that?"

Madam Love rubbed the sides of the pyramid. "It's an orgonite. Some people use it for healing or as a Feng Shui tool. It promotes tranquility and inner peace. It enhances my abilities to help others transform their lives for the better."

Colette leaned forward to inspect it. "Is that an amethyst inside?"

"Very good! There's also fine brass, copper, steel, aluminum and Dead Sea salt."

Lilly was convinced that Madam Love was a scam artist or a nut job. Orgonite? It sounded like a brand of suitcases or a citizen of Oregon.

Madam Love rubbed the pyramid again and her eyes widened. "I see great danger for you."

The absurdity of Madam Love's words made Lilly burst into laughter, followed by the involuntary swallowing of an entire piece of shrimp. She tried to breathe and had difficulty, the choking sensation getting worse by the second.

Lilly smacked the table and pointed to her throat.

Colette clapped her hands together. "Oh, I love this game! Okay, one word…"

Lilly's bulging eyes should have been a clue to Colette that this was a serious situation, not a game. Lilly shook her head and pointed to her throat again.

"You already told me that. One word—I know. Give me more. Is it a movie? I got it! *Deep Throat!*"

This is it. I'm going to die in a Panda Express. I didn't even get to finish my meal!

Madam Love reached over and karate-chopped Lilly on the back with the force of an aluminum baseball bat. The piece of shrimp flew out of her mouth, along with a few grains of fried rice, smacking Colette between the eyes.

Lilly coughed and gasped for air. Then she grabbed her glass of water, taking a large gulp.

"Please continue, Madam Love," Colette said, wiping her forehead as if nothing happened.

Lilly set down her water. "That's really not necessary. I'm not in any danger. You must be picking up vibes from someone else."

What was she saying? As if Lilly believed Madam Love really had magical powers but was just a little off course with her GPS.

Madam Love shook her head. "It's you. I feel it. Great, great danger…"

Right. Lilly had the safest life of anyone she knew. What sort of danger could she possibly encounter?

"Is there any way she can avoid the danger?" asked Colette, appearing to have bought the bull.

Lilly stood up and looked around the restaurant for hidden cameras. "Are we on one of those prank TV shows?"

Madam Love held up an index finger that appeared to be more like a warning. "Sit down and pay close attention. I will help you." She rubbed the pyramid a few more times. "Three things will happen and then you will be out of danger. Number one, you will see a bear."

Lilly laughed, grateful she had no food in her mouth this time. She eyed her keys in Colette's hand, waiting for the right moment to lunge for them again. She was so out of there.

"This is not a funny matter," said Madam Love as if she was telling Lilly to behave. "You will see a bear."

"A bear will help me get out of danger? Pardon me, but I think the bear *is* the danger. And how am I going to encounter a bear in the middle of a metropolitan city that has a population of a million people? Right…"

Madam Love ignored Lilly and continued, obviously having plenty of experience with non-believers. "Number two, you will go for a ride in a very expensive car."

"Okay, this is a general prediction that can happen to almost anyone. This is Silicon Valley. There are expensive cars parked at the secondhand stores. Not that big of a stretch."

Madam Love held up her finger again and Lilly noticed

the nail polish this time. A lovely purple that seemed to go well with her orange cape. "No, Lilly. Not your typical expensive car. Think another level above Mercedes and BMW. I mean *expensive* car."

"You going to give me a license plate number?"

"It doesn't work like that."

"It doesn't matter—I'm not impressed by material things, so you will *never* catch me in a car like that."

"And number three," she continued, ignoring Lilly once again. "I see you flying on a trip out of the country soon."

"Ha! Not even…"

A trip out of the country? Lilly couldn't believe what this crazy woman was saying. She was so far off base it wasn't even funny. If Madam Love had powers she would know that Lilly was scared of flying and had never been on an airplane. She had no plans to travel now or in the foreseeable future. Or for the rest of her life.

"And after these three things happen?" asked Colette. "She's safe?"

Madam Love nodded. "Then she will meet the man of her dreams. Her future husband."

Another shrimp flew out of Lilly's mouth, this time connecting with Madam Love's chest, before dropping to the front of her shirt.

Madam Love wiped her cape. "I really need to tell you these things when you're in between bites."

"It doesn't matter. I don't need to hear any more. There

11

are no bears anywhere close by. I don't ride in fancy cars. And I'm not going on any trips out of the country, so that eliminates your last prediction of me meeting a husband."

"Well…" Madam Love shrugged. "You could be right."

"See? You're already going back on what you said!"

Madam Love shook her head. "Not at all. I see a husband in your future. The man will make an appearance soon when you travel out of the country—I'm sure of it. Your soul mate. It will be up to *you* to do something about it —nobody can force you. You need to make that decision for yourself. But be warned…if you go against what is meant for you, if you try to fight it, you will suffer and continue to live a very unhappy life."

"Right!" Lilly said, wiping her mouth and taking another swig of water. "What you're telling me is crazy and has no chance of happening. I'm happy the way my life is at this moment." Madam Love just stared until Lilly felt uncomfortable. The woman was very good at intimidation but Lilly wouldn't stand for it. "Everything is fine."

Okay, maybe Lilly fibbed a little. Maybe she wasn't *perfectly* happy, but she wasn't *un*happy. Was she? Maybe she was, but Madam Love was grasping at straws. A bear? A trip out of the country? A husband? Right.

Madam Love placed the pyramid in her bag and stood. "My work is done here."

Colette paid Madam Love and hugged her. "Thank you so much for coming on short notice."

12

"My pleasure." She gestured to Lilly. "Your friend seems to want to resist nature. If she does it will be a huge mistake. You must encourage her to do the right thing."

Colette glared at Lilly. "I'll do my best."

Madam Love turned to walk away and then stopped. "I just picked up on something. It's just a word, but it's strong."

Colette took a step toward Madam Love. "What's the word?"

"Temple." She squeezed her eyes shut for a second and then opened them. "I'm not sure what it means, but there's a temple connected to the man Lilly will meet. Her future husband."

"Temple? What kind of temple? Like the temple on someone's head? Or temple like a church?"

Madam Love shrugged. "Just a temple. I don't know. That's all I got."

Colette glanced over to Lilly. "Remember that. A temple is important."

Lilly sighed. "It'll be at the top of my list. Just above *get milk and eggs at the grocery store.*" Madam Love left and Lilly shook her head. "Well, that was a waste of time. I can't believe you paid her for that. How much did she rip you off for?"

Colette stuck her wallet back in her purse. "It doesn't matter because you're worth it. I'm telling you, that woman is not a fake. Yes, there are plenty of scam artists in the world but she's not one of them."

"She's a crackpot."

"I guess we'll find out who's right and who's wrong, now won't we?"

"I guess we will."

They finished their meals in silence, Lilly's mind on Madam Love's predictions. It wasn't like she didn't want to have the love of her life, a husband, a marriage. But those dreams died a long time ago.

Chapter Two

To the untrained eye, the man on the other side of the bar might have appeared to know what he was talking about, but Marco Santini could spot a wine connoisseur imposter a mile away. He waited for the fake with the yellow polo shirt and the upturned collar to say something else that was complete and utter crap.

The man swished the wine around in his mouth like it was Listerine, then swallowed. "Although I prefer the effervescence and slight tongue tickle of a robust sparkling wine, I must say this one is really turning me on with its complex, full-bodied richness and slight underlying acidity."

He drained the rest of the wine, winked at his female companion, and held the glass out in front of Marco's face. "Keep it coming."

Fortunately, Marco was a patient man. He ignored the man's rudeness and poured him another sample. "This is our 2014 Merlot."

"Groovy, baby," the faker said doing the worst possible imitation of Austin Powers. His accent sounded more like Austin, Texas. But the guy was one hundred percent ostentatious.

This time he slurped the wine like hot tea and nodded. "The elegance of this Merlot is smooth on the palate and denotes a fruity bouquet of tantalizing sexiness." He pointed to the Pinot Noir. "Let me try some of that one over there."

"Of course. You can pour the rest of your glass into the spit bucket."

"Not on your life." The man slammed the rest of the wine and held the glass back out for Marco, who poured a sample of the Pinot.

As manager of Santander Winery, Marco had worked his way up in the company, learning every detail from every department. One of his job duties when he wasn't traveling for the company was to help out in the wine tasting room when they were short-staffed. He offered small samples from a list of wines produced by the winery.

Marco had seen all walks of life coming through the tasting room doors from wine snobs to imposters like this guy. Still, he wouldn't say a thing or embarrass the man. This was the exact person who would most likely buy a case or two of wine just to impress the girl.

"Sweet and supple," said the man, leaning toward the woman to kiss her. "Just like you, baby."

Oh God.

That was a new one.

Marco wanted to tell the woman to run for her life, but it wasn't his job to dispense relationship advice to strangers. Especially since he was far from an expert when it came to women.

The man dropped his credit card on the bar. "Give me two cases."

"You got it," Marco said, waiting until the guy's back was turned before rolling his eyes. Marco was grateful the man wanted to buy two cases, but he was tired of peddling someone else's wine. His dream was to be a winemaker—to sell his own wine.

Santander Winery had a good selection of wines but hadn't caught on like the more famous wineries just down the road on the Silverado Trail in Napa. Marco had ideas on how to improve many aspects of the winery's business but the owner didn't want to listen. Marco's boss was more interested in expanding to other countries instead of improving what he had first.

The man drained the rest of the wine in his glass. "Not bad. This one has a well-balanced, velvety structure that almost makes me want to dance naked on the bar. However, I feel there's a lack of sexiness in the tannenbaum."

"What are you talking about?" asked Jim Flanagan, Marco's boss and the owner of the winery.

Not good.

"Pardon me?" The man looked quite surprised that someone would call him on his bullshit.

Jim pointed to the man's empty glass on the bar. "Wine doesn't have tannenbaums. A tannenbaum is a German Christmas tree. Wine has *tannins*."

The color of the man's face was starting to resemble their 2015 Rose of Syrah. "That's what I said. I said tannins."

"No, you didn't."

"I did too."

The man and Jim had a stare-off and Marco moved in with a bottle of their best wine, hoping to smooth out the situation. "We don't bring this one out too often but please try our 2009 limited release Cabernet."

The man snagged his credit card from the bar and shoved it back in his wallet. "No thanks. You can forget about that purchase. We're out of here." He grabbed the woman's hand and marched toward the door, slamming it on the way out. A few seconds later Marco heard the sound of screeching tires in the parking lot.

"What?" said Jim, a look of innocence on his face.

Marco sighed and rubbed the back of his neck. "That guy wanted to buy two cases of wine before you showed up."

"We don't need people like that in here."

Marco grabbed the empty glasses from the bar and wiped down the counter. "Yes. We do. *Those people* keep the doors open and the business profitable, unlike that limo of college grads earlier whose only mission was to get drunk, not buy wine. They're the ones you should have turned away if you had to turn away someone." Marco gestured around the empty tasting room. "It's early in the day and we should be packed right now."

"I know, I know. I'll work on it. You know I'm not the greatest people person. Okay, change of topics—I need you to go back to Italy."

The man was crazy.

Marco had just gotten back from Rome three days earlier and still had jet lag. Plus he was leaving for Australia in less than two weeks to help build a new winery there. The project in Australia would keep him away from home for six months, so he wanted to use the time before the trip to see friends he hadn't seen in a while and relax.

"Don't look at me that way," Jim said, fidgeting with the bottle opener. "Dante's wife just went into labor a month early, so he can't go overseas now. You're the only other person I trust to make sure everything is ready to go at the exhibition."

Santander was a sponsor of the Lazio International Wine & Spirits Exhibition. It was all Jim had talked about for the last few months. It was an honor for the winery to be there but Marco wasn't in the mood to hop back on a plane so soon. He needed to convince Jim to send someone else.

"What about Robert?"

Jim shook his head. "No way."

"Steve?"

Jim stepped toward Marco and squeezed his shoulder. "You're my only option. I would go myself but the wife would kill me since that would mean missing our anniversary Caribbean cruise. We've had that trip planned for over a year and four other couples are going with us. Lucky for me you don't have a wife or a baby on the way."

Thanks for rubbing it in.

Not that Marco didn't want either but it made little sense with his lifestyle. What kind of family life would that be if he was never home?

No life at all.

That's why Marco had been avoiding women until he could get his career going in the right direction. This was also why he wanted to have his own business—so he could control everything and make all the decisions. So he could make other people do the traveling for him and only travel when it was for pleasure.

Marco didn't like this one bit and needed clarification. "So, you're telling me I need to fly to Rome, come back here for a few days, then turn around and go to Australia?"

"No, not at all. You'll fly to Rome to be at the event for opening day this Saturday. After you make sure everything is ready to go, you're free to do whatever you want until you continue on to Sydney. Hell, you always complain you don't get to enjoy the cities you travel to. Now's your chance."

"Jim…"

"I even picked up the hotel for the week even though you'll only be working one day. It was cheaper than flying you back here. Go visit your sister this time."

That part Marco wouldn't mind doing at all. He missed seeing Daniella and his best friend Stefano. But he also missed relaxing.

Marco placed two tasting bottles back on the shelf. "Okay."

What else could he say?

Jim slapped him on the back. "I knew I could count on you."

A few minutes later Marco called Stefano in Italy.

"Marco," said Stefano, answering on the first ring. "What's up, my friend?"

"Guess who's coming back to Italy?"

"What? Are you coming to Sorrento this time?"

"Yes. Finally. I can come see you when I'm done with work."

"Bellísimo! This is wonderful news. I'll tell Daniella."

Daniella was Stefano's wife, who also happened to be Marco's sister. Marco was the one who introduced the two of them and they were happily married.

Marco also wanted to be happily married.

"Are you there?" Stefano asked.

"Yeah. Sorry. I was thinking."

"Not a surprise. I'm serious when I tell you I want to move there and start a winery with you. California, here I come!"

Marco laughed, even though Stefano had the money to start such a venture if he wanted to. "Right. You have an amazing life in Sorrento. You're just going to pack up and leave that all behind?"

"Easily! I'm not defined by my job. Daniella is the most important thing in my life and I can love her the same, no matter where I live or what I do. Life is short and you have to follow your dreams. Look, we'll talk when you get here."

"Sounds good."

"And you need to meet a beautiful woman and have a family. Your clock is ticking."

Marco chuckled. "I don't know what types of books you've been reading but men don't have clocks. Give Daniella a kiss from me and I'll see you soon."

Marco ended the call, deep in thought. He was tired of his lifestyle and needed to make a change.

He was ready.

Chapter Three

Lilly reached over and stabbed the off button of the car stereo with her index finger when "Danger Zone" from Kenny Loggins came on. That was the last song she wanted to hear.

I see danger in your future.

The words from the psychic came right back to her. She tried to shake them out of her brain. She told herself that was just a coincidence, but she didn't want that song stuck in her head for the rest of the day.

Lunch with Colette and Madam Love was a complete waste of time. Not only did it break her out of her safe, normal routine, it irritated her since the psychic made the most ridiculous predictions. Lilly also didn't like that her best friend lied to her. She knew Colette was just trying to help, but did Lilly really need help? She didn't think so.

"Intervention," she mumbled to herself. "Right. I don't need no stinking intervention."

Lilly sat in her car at the corner, waiting for the light to change. She needed to get back to work where she felt safe. Plus, she had an important meeting to attend.

Something in her periphery from across the intersection

caught her attention. A mascot standing on the corner, waving a big sign promoting Bear River Pizza.

The mascot was a bear.

She leaned forward in her seat and roared with laughter, staring at the mascot through the windshield. Some psychic.

"A bear," she said to herself. "No way. That couldn't be what she was talking about."

The light turned green and Lilly drove her car across the intersection, cranking her head to the side, looking at the bear as she passed by.

"Just an idiotic coincidence," she said, putting her attention back on the road in front of her. But Lilly laughed so hard her car drifted to the side and before she could correct it, she drove it straight into the curb. The front tire exploded like a gunshot on impact. She applied the brakes and stuck the car in park, like she meant to put it there. This was why she didn't like to stray from her plan, her normal routine. Things happened. Bad things.

She let out a frustrated breath and got out of the car, walking around to the curbside. She confirmed the flat tire and shook her head. "Great."

Not good timing at all. She had to get back to a board of directors meeting in fifteen minutes and she didn't want to be late.

There was no time to call emergency roadside service— who knew how long that would take. She pulled out her cell phone to call Colette when she heard the sound of a horn.

She looked up and spotted a cherry red convertible Ferrari pulling over to the side.

An older woman waved through the open top and yelled. "Lilly!"

Lilly did a double-take when she realized who it was. Janet Mallery, the CEO of her company.

She stared at Janet's car.

A Ferrari.

A very expensive car.

Number two, you will go for a ride in a very expensive car.

Lilly paced back and forth on the sidewalk, talking to herself. "A bear. A very expensive car." She felt her pulse banging in her temple. "A bear. A very expensive car." She shook her head, no way.

"Lilly? You okay?"

Lilly turned around and forced a smile. "I'm not sure."

Janet approached and rubbed Lilly on the arm. "You don't look so hot. Do you hurt somewhere?"

"I'm not suffering from anything physical." She pointed to her head. "It's all up here."

"Ahh. Well, I think we all suffer from that." Janet chuckled and eyed the damage on Lilly's car. "You hit that curb hard but your car will be okay there." She pointed to her Ferrari. "Why don't you hop in? You don't want to be late for the meeting."

Lilly stared at Janet's car as fear struck her. Was she supposed to get in? That would make the psychic right on the first two predictions. Unless she didn't get in. Maybe she should call a taxi.

But be warned…if you go against what is meant for you, if you try to fight it, you will suffer greatly and continue to live a very unhappy life.

Damn that psychic and her words. This was all a coincidence.

"Lilly? We should be going. Don't worry, your car will be fine here."

"Okay." She grabbed her purse from the passenger seat, locked the car, and followed Janet to her Ferrari. She slid into the seat of the passenger side and inhaled the wonderful smell of the plush Italian leather. She glanced over at her boss. Some of the other employees had mentioned the sixty-year old woman had gotten the new car, but this was the first time she had seen it.

"We'd better step on it," said Janet. "We're going to be late."

"Of course."

Janet was already flying down the road as Lilly tried to strap herself in. She finally clicked the seatbelt into place and took a deep breath as Janet drove like a maniac to the office. How many laws did she break? Lilly had lost count. Speeding, failure to yield the right of way, running a red light, not coming to a complete stop, tailgating, improper lane change for starters.

After their arrival, she followed Janet to the third floor

where the other board members were already in the conference room waiting.

Lilly sat in between the CFO and the Vice President of Marketing. Janet walked to the white board in the front of the conference room, grabbed a red marker from the shelf and wrote on the whiteboard.

Roberto Rossi.

She circled his name, dropped the red marker back on the shelf and turned around.

"Okay," said Janet. "Sorry we're late. This will be quick but I wanted to make sure I had you all here for this." She pointed over her shoulder at the name on the board. "How many of you were here when Roberto Rossi worked with us?"

All the hands except for three went up. Lilly remembered Roberto since she was part of the initial screening process before he went through a series of interviews. Roberto was one of the best employees they had had until he was lured away with a big offer from another company. A good-looking man. Charming.

But why did Janet want to talk about Roberto? He obviously wasn't coming back to work for them because Lilly would have been one of the first to know about it.

"You know what a huge asset Roberto was to this company," Janet said, pacing in front of the seventy-inch monitor on the wall. "You also know that the product development team took a *huge* hit when he left. We thought we'd be able to recover when we brought in Erik, but we never even came close. So, now that Erik is on his way out, we want to—scratch that—*need to* get Roberto back in here on the team. ASAP."

"Isn't he living in Europe now?" asked Douglas, the Vice President of Engineering.

Janet nodded and reached across the solid red oak table, wiping dust from the Polycom conference phone. "Rome, to be exact. And I need someone to fly there and drag his butt back here."

Laughter filled the room.

Janet kept a straight face. "I'm serious. I tried to get him to come back, but he turned down my offer. And he hasn't returned subsequent emails and phone calls. Word has it he's ready to sign a contract with Samsung. I need a volunteer to fly to Rome and wine and dine Roberto until he says yes. We'll pay him thirty percent more than the Samsung offer." She glanced around the room, making eye contact with every single person. "Who will do it?"

It only took a few seconds before the psychic's words popped right back into Lilly's head again.

I see you going on a trip out of the country and meeting the man of your dreams. Your future husband.

Was this the opportunity Madam Love talked about? Was Roberto Rossi the man of her dreams? Her future husband?

"This is crazy," said Lilly, digging her fingernails into the padded leather arms of the chair.

"Not that crazy at all," answered Janet, thinking Lilly was talking to her. "Sometimes you have to be proactive. Forget about the horns, it's time to grab the bull by the balls. Well, not you, Lilly. I know you don't fly, so I've already ruled you out for this." Janet surveyed the room, waiting for someone to say yes.

Everyone sat there.

This couldn't be what the psychic was talking about, could it? Was she supposed to volunteer? Her heart rate picked up as she considered the possibility.

No way. This was crazy. There was no way she could fly to Rome for God knows how many hours. A one-hour flight was sixty minutes too much. This had to be a coincidence but Lilly wasn't feeling well.

If you go against what is meant for you, if you try to fight it, you will suffer greatly and continue to live a very unhappy life.

Lilly stood and took a few deep breaths.

Janet took a few steps toward her. "Are you okay, Lilly?"

The room started to spin, and the temperature was rising.

Lilly grabbed the edge of the table. "I don't feel so good."

Lilly stared up from her back on the floor at Janet, who

hovered over her. Her brain was cloudy, but she was relaxed —like she awoke from a nap. "What happened? Why am I on the floor?"

"You passed out," Janet said, fanning her with a folder.

Lilly blinked twice. "Wow. Okay."

Fortunately, the company was big enough to have a paramedic on staff and she arrived within two minutes to make sure Lilly was okay.

Then it all came back to her.

The Bear. The Ferrari. Italy.

The psychic was right. Lilly couldn't fight it. She'd fallen for her last boyfriend and then he'd split on her. She'd placed all her hopes on him and when he dropped out of sight, she went into self-imposed exile. How could she have let a man do that to her? The wake-up call from the psychic snapped her out of her stupidity! She'd wasted three years for nothing. She didn't want to be unhappy for the rest of her life. She wanted what every other person wanted.

To love and to be loved.

All of her friends were married. If the third prediction was true and she had to leave the country to meet her future husband, then she would do it! Her fear of flying was a huge issue but people took tranquilizers for that, right? No more hiding from life. No more just going through the motions.

Suddenly her adrenaline was pumping. She felt alive. She was on a mission. She would volunteer to go to Rome, bring back Roberto, the man of her dreams.

Wait a minute.

Could Roberto really be the man of her dreams? She hadn't seen him in years but did remember he was attractive. Sweet too. She didn't know him well, but there was no need to worry about that at the moment. It was time to take action.

Lilly stretched her arms out. "Okay, I'm ready to get up."

Janet and the paramedic grabbed Lilly by the arms and helped her to her feet. They guided her to the chair to sit for a moment until she felt okay to walk. She felt much better. She smoothed out her clothes and took a deep breath.

"You sure you're okay?" asked Janet, handing her a bottle of water.

Lilly nodded, opened the bottle, and took a swig. "Yeah. Much better." This was it. She had to do it. "And I want to volunteer to go to Rome to bring back Roberto."

Janet jerked her head back, analyzed Lilly for a moment, and then gripped Lilly by the shoulders. "Did you hit your head?"

Lilly laughed. "I know, I know. The girl who doesn't like to fly or do anything wants to go to Rome."

Janet laughed along with her. "Maybe you should pass out more often because I like this new you. But I'm afraid you won't be able to go to Rome."

She wasn't expecting that response. "I don't understand. You wanted a volunteer. You changed your mind?"

"No, no. Not at all. William already volunteered."

Lilly scanned the room for William but he was gone. In fact, almost everyone else had left.

After drinking more water and assuring Janet and the medical staff she was okay, Lilly headed back to her office and closed the door behind her.

She leaned against the back of the door, staring across her office at the African violet on the windowsill that desperately needed water. She moved in that direction and emptied the rest of her water bottle in the soil, deep in thought.

Something didn't feel right.

Like maybe she'd messed up and William had stolen her opportunity. What could she do? She had her chance and blew it. Was that it? Was she going to be unhappy for the rest of her life?

A few seconds later she called Colette.

"Does this mean you forgive me?" answered Colette.

"The psychic was right. The bear. The Ferrari. And also —"

"You saw a bear?"

"Yes. No. Well, kind of. Colette, something freaky is going on. They offered us a chance to go to Rome to recruit Roberto, a former employee."

"Yes! I told you Madam Love was amazing. See how everything lined up for you? Do it! Go to Rome and meet your future husband. It must be Roberto."

Lilly sighed. "That's just it. I tried but William beat me to it."

"No! Don't you dare let that happen. You march right into William's office and tell him *you* are the one who needs to go to Italy. Offer him your body if you have to."

"Very funny."

"Okay, don't offer him your body, even though it might do you some good. Just go talk with him *now*. Convince him not to go. The writing is on the wall, sweetie. If you don't go on that trip, you may regret this for the rest of your life."

Chapter Four

"I think I'm going to pee myself right here in the airport," said the woman talking on her cell phone next to Marco. "Then I'll probably pee myself again when I get on the plane."

He scooted over as much as he could since their chairs were connected. Better safe than sorry. Hopefully they wouldn't be seated next to each other on the flight.

Marco turned to get a look at the woman who had no problem sharing her bodily function issues with everyone at Gate 18. Attractive. Around thirty. Big brown eyes that matched her hair. She wore snug black pants and a yellow blouse. She looked like a bumblebee.

A bumblebee with a bladder problem.

"I just need to get to Rome without dying," she continued.

Scratch that. A *dramatic* bumblebee with a bladder problem.

"Then I'll find Roberto and drag him back here."

Maybe she's a bounty hunter.

Marco cleared his throat, hoping to get the woman to lower her voice. He didn't like to listen to other people's conversations.

"Colette, listen. You've flown a thousand times. This is my first time!"

Now it made sense. It was amazing how many people had a fear of flying. Marco had been one of them long ago, but he learned a few tricks and the anxiety went away.

"Thank you for waiting, ladies and gentleman," said the airline employee on the PA system behind the ticket counter. "We would like to continue the pre-boarding process for Flight 5479 to Washington DC with continuing service to Rome. We invite first class passengers and Platinum members to board at this time."

Marco stood and grabbed hold of his carry-on. He rolled it toward the ticket agent and was sideswiped by Miss Drama-Weak-Bladder-Bounty-Hunter-Bumble-Bee and her angry carryon. She didn't say a word and continued, stopping in front of the ticket agent.

The woman fumbled with her boarding pass and dropped it, along with her ID and several other items. "So sorry."

"Not a problem at all," said the agent. "Take your time."

Marco bent down to pick up her library card, checking out her name before handing it to her.

Lilliana Jones.

She scrambled to pick up the rest of her items. "Okay, okay. Here you go." She handed the agent the boarding pass. "I also have my passport and social security card."

Rich Amooi

Marco chuckled. "Don't forget the library card."

The woman gave Marco a look like she was annoyed with him helping. Either that or she was embarrassed that he saw her library card. He could always flash his own library card to make her feel better, but he opted to just keep quiet.

"You don't need any of that since you already passed through security," said the agent, scanning the woman's boarding pass and waving her through. "Enjoy your flight."

A few minutes later, Marco entered the first class cabin and stopped behind Miss Library Card. She opened the overhead compartment and grabbed her bag from the floor.

Marco reached for her bag to help. "I can get that."

"I can handle it," said the woman, bending down, grabbing the bag, and sliding it into the overhead compartment. She took a seat as Marco lifted his bag and placed it next to hers.

He sat next to her and smiled. "I'm Marco."

"Lilly."

He nodded and grinned. "One of my favorite wines is named after you."

"Excuse me?"

"Lilly Pilly. It's a family owned boutique winery in Australia. I'm going there next week. I don't drink a lot of sweet wine but I drink theirs. Lilly Pilly. Good stuff."

"Thanks for sharing, Marco Polo." She tucked some hair behind one of her ears and shrugged. "One of my favorite childhood games is named after you..." She clasped her

36

seatbelt and pulled the excess belt tighter.

"Lots of things rhyme with Lilly. Silly. Frilly. Chili." Marco had a habit of rambling around good-looking women and Lilly would fit in that category. She reminded him of Sandra Bullock in the movie *While You Were Sleeping*.

Quirky. Beautiful.

Lilly unclasped the seatbelt and did it again. And again.

"Nervous, Lilly?" asked Marco.

She kept her eyes on a passenger walking down the aisle and waiting for him to pass before she whispered to Marco. "Terrified."

The flight attendant stopped at Marco's side and smiled. "Care for a pre-flight drink?"

"Coffee with sugar," Lilly said.

"You got it. You, sir?"

"I'll have the Gnarly Head cabernet." He held up his index finger. "Just a moment…"

"Of course."

Marco leaned into Lilly. "Caffeine exacerbates anxiety. Have a glass of wine instead."

Lilly stared at Marco for a few seconds and then raised her gaze back up to the flight attendant. "I changed my mind. Can I have the…" She glanced at Marco. "What did you order?"

"Gnarly Head."

Lilly nodded. "I'll have the same."

"You got it," said the flight attendant, walking away.

Marco turned to Lilly. "Channel fourteen on the audio entertainment has soothing music, in case you need it."

She nodded. "Thank you. Sounds like you fly a lot."

"A little too much."

"Business?"

"Yup. Rome for a few days. Then Australia for six months."

"Wow. What do you do for a living?"

"I'm general manager of a winery."

"Ahh. I get it. You're pushing the wine because it's your livelihood."

Marco chuckled. "Yeah. Because that extra glass you ordered should keep the wine industry going strong for another year." He laughed again. "What about you? Flying for business?"

"Uh...kind of."

Marco waited for her to say something else but she opted to keep quiet.

Twenty minutes later the captain made the announcement. "Flight attendants please prepare for take-off."

"Oh God," said Lilly. "This is it." She slammed back the rest of her wine and grabbed the headphones from the seat-back pocket, slipping them over her head. She pressed her body back in her seat and turned up the music.

Lilly closed her eyes, gripped one arm rest with her left hand, and latched onto Marco's forearm with her right hand.

Marco peeked to the left. She had her eyes closed. Could she possibly think his arm was the armrest?

Holy crap, this woman has got the grip from hell.

"Uh…Lilly?"

She didn't answer. She kept her eyes closed, her body rigid, listening to the music in her headphones. It looked like she was trying to psych herself out and get distracted.

And his arm was paying the price.

He would have never thought that a woman her size would have that type of strength. The pain was becoming unbearable, but he didn't want to say anything since the plane was moving, almost airborne. This was helping her cope with her fear of flying. He'd worry about all the damage from the lack of circulation in his arm and her embedded fingernails later.

The airplane left the ground, and she squeezed his arm even tighter.

God. She's like a boa constrictor, trying to cut off the blood supply to my hand.

"I don't want to die," Lilly said, yanking the headphones from her head and taking deep breaths.

Marco glanced over and spoke through his gritted teeth, not able to take it anymore. "I'm the one who will die if you don't let go of my arm."

She opened her eyes. "What are you talking about?"

Marco pointed to her hand squeezing his arm. "Your death grip. You're killing me."

<<<>>>

Lilly looked down and realized she had been squeezing Marco's arm instead of the armrest. She released his arm and inspected it. It was red and purple and looked like it had been passed through a meat grinder.

"Oh my God," Lilly said, grimacing. "I'm so sorry."

Marco lifted his arm and winced. He opened and closed his fist a few times and stretched his arm out in front of him. Then he rubbed his arm and frowned. "Remind me never to arm wrestle you or get on your bad side."

Lilly snorted and threw her hand over her mouth.

"Great. Now you're laughing at me."

"Sorry." She laughed again. "It's horrible what I did to your arm but funny too, you have to admit."

"I don't see the humor." He opened and closed his fist again. "At least the feeling is coming back."

The flight attendant returned with more wine. "Refill?"

Marco and Lilly both said yes.

Lilly couldn't believe what she had done to Marco. Especially after he had been so kind in recommending the wine and relaxing music. She felt powerful. She had no idea she could cause so much damage. Oddly enough, she felt much better.

She looked around the plane and then opened the window shade. They were in the air. And she was okay.

"I can't believe it."

Marco chuckled. "I can't either."

"No, not your arm. Well, I can't believe that either but I'm talking about the plane. We're flying."

"That we are."

"And I didn't freak out."

"I would like to disagree with you one thousand percent."

"Seriously. Yes, I mangled your arm, but I expected to scream and cry like a baby and pee myself. And I didn't." She turned to Marco. "Thank you."

"I didn't do anything."

"Yes, you did. You distracted me. And I can't believe you said nothing when I grabbed your arm."

He shrugged. "Just trying to help…"

Lilly didn't know the man, but it was obvious he was a good person. She casually glanced over. She had been so filled with anxiety she didn't even realize how good-looking he was. The typical woman's dream man. Tall, dark, and handsome. She dropped her gaze down to his torn-apart arm regaining its natural color. Then checked out his fingernails.

Well-groomed. She liked that.

He lifted his arm and surveyed the damage again. "It'll be okay. I was mauled by a bear once and this was a little better than that."

She laughed and her thoughts drifted to the psychic and

her prediction of the bear. Funny how things changed so quickly. She was convinced in her mind she would never travel on a plane and there she was on the way to Rome. Everything the psychic had predicted so far had come true. The bear. The expensive car. Traveling out of the country. The only thing left was meeting her future husband. She glanced over at Marco again.

It can't be him. He travels for a living and will be in Australia for months.

After the meal service, Marco stood to let Lilly out of her seat to use the restroom. She slid from between the seats and hit her leg on the last armrest, wobbling and grabbing Marco's shoulders to keep from falling.

Marco grabbed her by the waist to stabilize her, a concerned look on his face. "You okay?"

She forced a smile. "Yeah. I didn't feel the full effect of the three glasses of wine until I stood up." She looked down at his hands on her waist and raised her gaze until their eyes met. "Uh…thank you. I should be fine."

He removed his hands from her waist. "Of course. I'm here if you need a designated walker."

Marco glanced at Lilly who was now out cold. She had fallen asleep after she had returned from the bathroom. Not a surprise since she had three glasses of wine.

What a beautiful sight to see. So peaceful. He was curious about the woman. She seemed like a decent person —maybe had issues and baggage like most people, but there was nothing wrong with that. Hell, he had things he had to deal with in his own life. But when she didn't speak—didn't move—there was something angelic about her.

Lilly pulled the blanket up closer to her chin. "Nice to meet you."

Marco did a double take. "Nice to meet you too."

Lilly's eyes were still closed, and she said nothing else. Odd. They had been talking for over three hours so why did she say it was nice to meet him now? You'd think she'd say that after they went their separate ways in Rome. Maybe she was just having fun with him.

"I saw a bear," she said. "And I rode in an expensive car."

"Are you messing around?" he asked. "Very funny."

No answer.

Maybe she was talking in her sleep. Lots of people did that. He sat back and closed his eyes. The thought of sleeping for a little sounded like a great idea.

"I'm going to meet my future husband in Italy."

Marco opened his eyes and turned to Lilly again. He sat up in his seat and peeked over toward her left hand resting on her lap. He didn't see an engagement ring on her finger, so meeting a future husband made no sense at all. Besides, she would have said fiancé, not future husband. Unless it was an arranged marriage, and she hadn't met the guy yet. Who knew how that worked? Maybe the wedding was in Italy—a destination wedding. Was she a mail-order bride? Marco pictured someone packing Lilly in a box and shipping her to Italy.

He chuckled. "That would be funny."

"I don't speak Italian," said Lilly. "Yes, I would love a cappuccino. Two sugars please. Will you marry me?"

"Lilly?" he whispered. "Can you hear me?"

"Yes."

"You can?"

Lilly moved her head like she was trying to find a more comfortable position. "You're very attractive."

Marco raised an eyebrow. "Uh…okay. I think you're—"

"A spring wedding sounds lovely."

"Huh?"

Marco moved closer to her, trying to figure out if she was playing around with him. She smelled fantastic. Like roses, with a hint of gummi bears.

Lilly was obviously talking in her sleep. It was fascinating to hear what she was saying, but he felt a little guilty. Like she was revealing private information, and he was eavesdropping. It's not like he went out of his way to listen—they were sitting next to each other.

A minute later she opened her eyes.

"Nice nap?" he asked, hoping she didn't think he was checking her out while she slept.

She sat up and stretched her arms out. "Yeah. I was a zombie there for a while."

He nodded. "I've been in that state before. That's when you get the most vivid dreams, I think."

"Uh-huh."

"Did you have sweet dreams?"

She squished her eyebrows together. "Kind of odd question, don't you think?"

"Not at all, people dream. What do you remember?"

She shook her head and pointed to his face. "You look suspicious and—" She stared at him for a few more seconds. "Oh God. Was I talking in my sleep? Please tell me no."

"No."

She analyzed him again. "Okay, please tell me the truth."

He grinned. "Yes."

"Ahhh!"

He loved the color of her embarrassed cheeks but didn't want to torture her. "It wasn't so bad."

"I don't want to know. Well I do, but I don't."

"You'd be disappointed if I told you, so maybe it's best we keep it my little secret.

"Okay, now I have to know."

"I'll tell you then. On the layover."

"What? No, no, no. I don't have the patience for that."

The fasten seatbelt light illuminated, followed by a ding over the PA system of the airplane.

"Ladies and gentleman, as we begin our descent into Washington DC, we'd like to ask you to please fasten your seat belts and bring your seat backs and tray tables to their upright and locked positions. We'll be coming around the cabin one last time to collect any trash you may have. We'll be on the ground shortly."

Marco pointed to the overhead speakers. "Darn, I was just about to tell you. Okay, it'll have to wait. We have a three-hour layover, so I can tell you in the airport. Are you going to grab a snack or drink in the terminal?"

"Uh…I guess."

"Good. It's a date."

"A date?"

"Relax. It's just a figure of speech."

Not that he wouldn't mind going out with Lilly. She was beautiful and had a fun personality when she wasn't freaking out. But pursuing Lilly, or any woman, wasn't going to happen.

Chapter Five

Lilly nibbled on her quesadilla at the food court inside the Washington Dulles International Airport. Marco ate his grilled chicken burrito and looked up and smiled in between bites. They had about two hours before they had to return to the terminal to take the second leg of the flight from DC to Rome.

Lilly couldn't believe she talked in her sleep on the airplane. She'd been doing that ever since she was a little girl in elementary school but the last thing she wanted to do was do it in front of a stranger. Especially a good-looking one. Plenty of people had made fun of her over the years. Family, kids at summer camp, friends, past boyfriends—you name it. She wondered if Marco would do the same.

It wouldn't have been so bad if she could control what came out of her mouth because most of the time it was the most random and bizarre thing. Other times it was exactly what was on her mind before she fell asleep and that's what worried her because she had been thinking about the psychic. She would die of embarrassment if Marco found out she was on a mission to find a husband in Italy, besides bring back Roberto.

"Okay, you've had your fun," she said. "Tell me everything I said while I slept."

Marco took a sip of his water, the entire time his eyes never leaving Lilly. "Okay. Here's what I heard. Ready?"

"Ready."

"Okay." Marco analyzed her for a moment and swallowed hard. "You like unicorns and caramel corn and stuffed monkeys."

Lilly stared at him. "I didn't say that."

"How do you know if you were sleeping?"

"First, I have a fear of being stabbed to death by a unicorn. He chases me down a beach and I trip. I turn over, so I can see him and before I can say a word he thrusts forward and repeatedly stabs me in the heart. Second, however tasty it may be, caramel corn sticks to my teeth and I have this fear of my mouth not being able to open after I chew on some. I can't breathe and I die."

"Why don't you breathe through your nose?"

"Allergies."

"Ahhh. And the stuffed monkeys?"

She shrugged. "They can be cute. Unless they are the kind that come to life and try to strangle you while you sleep."

Marco laughed. "You have a wild imagination. You also seem to be scared of a lot of things, especially dying." He grabbed a chip and dipped it in salsa. "Are you going to have time to see some things in Rome or is your trip strictly business?"

"Very smooth how you changed the subject. We haven't finished discussing what I said in my sleep."

"Yes, we finished."

"That's it?"

"That's it. Tell me about your plans when you get to Rome."

Lilly took the last bite of her quesadilla and held up her index finger as she pulled her carryon closer. She unzipped the large compartment and pulled out her books. "I've done my research and have everything planned down to the hour." She made space on the table and arranged the books in alphabetical order. *Fodor's Italy. Italy Travel Guide. Lonely Planet Italy. Rick Steves Italy.*

Marco blinked. "You're joking."

"Why would I joke about something like that?" She unfolded her day-to-day itinerary and eyed the table. "Running out of room here." She scooted his burrito off to the side, along with the chips and salsa. "Better. Okay, I will hit the ground running when we land. This is what I have planned after I drop the bags off at the hotel."

Lilly was proud of her plan. She had spent almost fourteen hours working on it and could see all the most popular tourist attractions easily. She should be a travel planner.

Marco leaned in to inspect her masterpiece itinerary, shaking his head. "This is pathetic."

Lilly cranked her head around and huffed. "What? You can't be serious. This is a traveler's dream. Having everything planned out like this took time and hard work but will ensure that I see *everything* I have to see."

"Not even. You'll burn out on the first day because you didn't take jet lag into consideration. This is the most ridiculous way to travel. You have everything scheduled down to the hour. Restaurants. Tourist traps. Souvenir shops." He laughed and pointed at the itinerary. "You even have the bathroom breaks scheduled. Oh, that's right. You have a tendency to pee your pants. I remember now, so maybe those are necessary."

"Very funny. Admit it. I'm well-prepared and you're jealous."

He pointed to the itinerary again. "This is no way to see the beautiful country where my ancestors came from. I already see a big flaw in your plan on the very first day that will throw off the itinerary for the entire week."

Lilly analyzed her schedule for the first day. Everything looked just the way it should be to her. "What are you talking about? This is perfect."

Marco shook his head and placed his finger on the first item on the list. "The Pantheon should not be the first thing you see."

She stared down at his well-groomed finger. "Why not?"

"Once you see in person with your very own eyes the majestic, beautiful, fascinating, historical Colosseum, you'll want to visit it *immediately*. But *you* have it scheduled on…" He scanned the itinerary. "Day four! This will drive you crazy. Every time you see the Colosseum, every time you walk by it, every time you hear someone mention it, you will kick yourself for not scheduling it on the first day. Your first mistake."

"Well, I have patience and think you're exaggerating. What's my second mistake?"

"You chose the most touristy restaurants to eat in. These are not the true Italy. These are food factories designed to shuffle people in and out as fast as possible. Their menus feature plates fast to prepare, so you can eat and be on your way. You're missing out on some of the best places to eat."

"I've done the research. Many of these places have good reviews."

"From people like you. You won't find the locals eating at these places. You should go where the locals go to eat. *That* is the real Italy."

"I'm sure I'll have no problem enjoying the food. I'm not that picky."

Marco snorted.

"Hey!" said Lilly, crossing her arms. "You barely even know me, so don't judge."

"Fine." He pointed to something else on her list of things to do. "This is ridiculous and an impossibility."

She leaned down again to see what his finger was sitting on. "What's wrong with doing a church and temple tour? I love to see the architecture and the stained glass." She'd also love to find her future husband inside one of those temples but she wasn't going to tell Marco that.

"There's nothing wrong with it at all, but you've allotted three hours for this. There are over nine hundred churches in Rome."

Lilly blinked. "Nine hundred. Wow. Okay, anything else?"

Marco shook his head. "If I tell you, are you going to change things on your itinerary?"

"No. Everything is planned and I don't stray from the plan."

"Ever?"

"Ever!"

Marco chuckled. "So you don't like spontaneity?" He pointed to her face. "Why did you cringe when I mentioned spontaneity? There—you cringed again."

"I don't know what you're talking about," she lied, wishing there was something she could hide behind.

"If you say so… I recall a certain woman sitting next to me on the plane who changed her drink order from coffee to wine once she was shown the error of her decision. That was spontaneous. Sound familiar?"

"Can't say it does," Lilly said, for a total of two lies in less than a minute.

"Not a surprise." He folded the itinerary back up for Lilly and handed it to her. "Your planning is faulty and designed to fail. This is no way to see Italy and you're spending almost all of your time in Rome. The city is magnificent, but there is so much you'll miss. If you want to see Italy the right way, the way it was meant to be enjoyed and remembered and treasured, I would be happy to show you."

Lilly laughed. "You?"

"Yeah. Me."

"I thought you were here for work?"

"Just for one day. Then I'm free for a few days before I go to Australia."

How crazy would that be to have her own personal tour guide? A *handsome* tour guide? This was a tempting offer. But how could she meet her future husband if she was with Marco the entire time? It would defeat the purpose if Italian men stayed away from her because they thought she was taken.

Unless Roberto was her man.

In that case, maybe she could just have fun with Marco until she met up with Roberto.

No.

Too much risk for not enough gain.

"Well?" asked Marco.

Lilly gathered her books and stuck them back in her carryon. "No, thank you."

"Can I ask you why you don't like to improvise?"

"Yes, you can. I just won't tell you why." Lilly didn't like how that came out of her mouth. She sounded kind of bitchy and it wasn't fair to Marco. The guy did nothing at all. He'd been kind and helpful, even though he picked apart her plan. "Sorry. I don't like the way I answered you, so I apologize. I'd rather not talk about it."

"As you wish."

They made their way back to the gate, not saying a word to each other. Lilly had a feeling she'd hurt Marco's feelings. She felt bad, but she didn't want to talk about being spontaneous. She had enough of those talks with Colette.

On the flight from DC to Rome, Marco moved to the empty seat next to Lilly. Obviously he wasn't mad at her for her behavior. She chatted with him for over two hours about life, work, and travel. In fact, she rather enjoyed Marco's company. He was easy to talk to and easy on the eyes. They even laughed their way through the movie *Hitch* on their own personal screens.

After the movie, Lilly was getting sleepy but kept herself awake until she heard Marco snoring. Then she closed her eyes and drifted off. She didn't want to take a chance of Marco hearing her talk in her sleep again.

After they landed in Rome, went through immigration, and grabbed their bags, they headed toward the ground transportation.

"Where are you staying?" Marco asked.

"Palazzo Manfredi."

Marco jerked his head back.

"What?" asked Lilly. "I didn't say it right?"

"Your pronunciation was *perfecta*," he said, emphasizing the last word with a beautiful Italian accent. "It's just the hotel you're staying at is an amazing place and many of the rooms have a view of the Colosseum. Never stayed there before but I had dinner in their rooftop restaurant once. Benissimo!"

"How come you're suddenly sounding more Italian to me?"

Marco laughed. "This happens when I arrive. I crank up my Italian button and presto!"

Lilly laughed. "I like it."

"So glad. Hey, do you want to share a taxi? My hotel is just down the street from yours."

"Sounds great."

They rolled their bags over to the taxi area and a few minutes later they were on the way to the hotels.

As they pulled up to Lilly's hotel, her mouth dropped open. They must have been fifty feet from the Colosseum. She continued to stare out the window in awe.

Marco smiled. "The offer is still open. I can show you Rome. Or you can get stressed out like most tourists and pass out in your hotel room each night, kicking yourself for not taking me up on my offer. Your choice."

Lilly laughed. "Thank you but now I have to do it my way just to prove you wrong."

"So be it." He pulled the wallet from his pocket and

handed her his business card. "If you change your mind. Or if you'd like to stay in touch. I have international service on my phone, so call me anytime." He smiled and opened the door to get out with her. The driver pulled her bags out. Lilly pulled her wallet from her purse and Marco waved her off. "It's a flat rate and I'm the last stop, so I'll take care of it."

She stuck her wallet back in her purse and held out her hand. "Thank you, Marco. It was a pleasure meeting you."

He stared at her hand for a moment and then accepted it. "A pleasure to meet you too, but you're in Italy now and this is how we do it." He pulled her closer and kissed her on both cheeks.

Ooh. Can you do that again?

He continued to hold on to her hand for a few seconds longer and kept eye contact. "Goodbye, Lilly Pilly."

"Goodbye, Marco Polo."

He let go over her hand and pointed to the Colosseum. "And good luck with that!" He laughed and got back in the taxi.

Lilly watched the taxi zoom away, forgetting for that brief moment she was in Italy. She had forgotten about the Colosseum that was only a few feet away. Her mind was focused on his kisses. It was a simple, innocent gesture, but why did she enjoy it so much? And why did she wonder if she was making a mistake by not taking him up on his offer?

Chapter Six

"Marco was right." Lilly stared out the hotel room window at the Colosseum. There it was, the most popular tourist attraction in all of Italy right before her eyes.

Calling her. Taunting her. Waving her over.

Lilly wanted to go inside at that moment, but would have to wait four days to see it. She shook her head and unpacked. She wouldn't feel good going out to see Rome, knowing that everything was still in her suitcase.

Lilly unpacked, then made a phone call to Roberto to meet the next day for coffee at four in the afternoon. Roberto was happy to hear from her, which was a great sign.

If everything went according to plan she would just need an hour or two to convince him to come back to the States and join her team again. She needed to make him an offer he couldn't refuse.

Lilly left the hotel toward her first tourist attraction, a Roman temple called the Pantheon. Could her future husband be there waiting inside for her? Only time would tell.

It was only a twenty-minute walk to the Pantheon, and it felt great to move and stretch. She was thirty minutes behind schedule, which wasn't too bad, considering how crowded the city was and the amount of traffic. She could make up that time and then some during the rest of her church/temple tour after the Pantheon.

As she strolled down Via dei Fori Imperialli, she took a few deep breaths and tried to get adjusted to being in another country. She couldn't believe she was in Italy. The streets were jammed with cars and taxis, all of them moving back and forth from one lane to the other like they couldn't make up their minds. How the people driving the scooters weren't killed on a daily basis was beyond her. Not to mention the people. This city was alive, but she needed to be careful.

Everywhere she looked there were churches with the most exquisite stained glass, domes painted white, gray or gold, pillars in front of most buildings, statues of Gods and famous Romans, and fountains. Fountains everywhere.

She wanted to stop at least fifteen or twenty times along the way to the Pantheon, but knew she couldn't or it would throw off her entire schedule. A little farther down she made a left on Piazza della Madonna di Loreto and continued walking. A few minutes later she stopped in Piazza di Venezia and stared at an immense white marble monument.

Lilly checked her notes and realized this one was called Il Vittoriano, a monument dedicated to the first king of Italy. It was gorgeous. She couldn't stay but she pulled out her camera and snapped a quick picture.

"Beautiful," she said to herself.

"Bella!" said the male voice with a thick Italian accent behind her.

Lilly studied basic Italian expressions before the trip and knew that *bella* meant *beautiful*. Obviously the man was agreeing with her—it was an impressive monument.

"Bella, bella."

Okay, maybe he was a little more emphatic than she was but she had heard that the Italians were almost as passionate as the Spaniards.

She flipped around and stared at the smiling man who wasn't looking at the monument. He was looking at her. He wore white pants and a matching white cotton jacket. His light blue shirt had three buttons open at the top, exposing a little too much chest hair for her liking. The sports watch on his wrist was so large it could have doubled as a kitchen wall clock.

He slid his sunglasses down his nose a little, whistling and taking his time to check out Lilly from head to toe. "Bella, where have you been all my life?"

"California."

His eyes grew wide. "California! This is wonderful! I have been expecting you. Welcome."

"Thank you."

Lilly stared at him for a moment. This couldn't be her future husband. No way could it be that easy. Not that he was bad-looking at all. Except for the giant patch of hair exploding out of his open shirt, he was handsome and even had a little bit of sexy stubble. But how was she to know when she'd meet her future husband? Madam Love mentioned nothing about that.

Most likely this guy was just one of the typical Italian guys she had read about. Someone who hits on anything that moves. But she didn't want to just blow him off without knowing for sure. Maybe she would have to wait for a sign to know if he was the one. Hopefully she wouldn't have to wait too long because she had things to do and didn't want to waste time with someone she knew wouldn't be a part of her future.

"I have a girlfriend," he said. "But today, for you, no girlfriend."

The sign couldn't have been any clearer. She told him *no way in hell* with the shake of her head and continued walking. She suspected she would have to put up with more of that but it came with the territory.

"I want to make love to you," he yelled from behind her.

She stopped and turned around. "And what about your girlfriend?"

He thought about it for a moment. "You mean you want her to join us?"

She huffed, turned her back on the man and continued her walk toward the Pantheon.

"Can I get you a hot drink to melt the ice?" he yelled.

Lilly ignored him and pressed forward. A few minutes

later she passed between the huge marble columns and two giant bronze doors of the Pantheon. She headed to the middle, stopped, and stared up into the largest unreinforced concrete dome in the world. She was in awe of the architectural geniuses who built this masterpiece almost two thousand years ago and marveled at how it was still one of the best preserved of all ancient Roman buildings.

It didn't take long before her mind was on men. *Man,* to be more specific. Too bad all the men inside the Pantheon were with women. She wasn't going to meet anyone there.

Twenty minutes later Lilly couldn't understand how she was further off schedule. It made little sense at all, but she had to go already, getting a little stressed out.

Lilly slid between an older couple and headed right back out. So much for enjoying the second most visited tourist stop in Rome. But what came next was even worse. Lilly's plans came to a screeching halt when she arrived at a cathedral and it was closed.

She hurried to the next church, and it was closed as well.

"I don't get it," she said to herself.

Madam Love's words popped back into her head.

There's a temple connected to the man Lilly will meet. Her future husband.

She wasn't expecting it to be so difficult.

Lilly sat on a bench in front of a nut shop and searched through one of the travel guides. She found out the majority of the churches and temples weren't even open after seven in the evening. What happened?

She knew exactly what happened.

She'd carefully done research but forgot to check the hours of operation! Amazing. She was suddenly tired and frustrated. She bought a bag of cashews from the nut shop and walked back toward the hotel, unexpectedly thinking of Marco.

A cute couple walked in her direction, hand in hand, smiling, kissing. Like they didn't have a care in the world.

She wanted that.

Not only someone to enjoy Italy with but to enjoy life with. She wasn't that picky.

Lilly wanted someone she connected with. Someone she was attracted to, but most importantly, someone she could have great conversations with. Because if the physical attraction ever wore off or their body parts ever drooped so low they were unusable, at least she'd still be able to enjoy the company of the other person.

Her first evening in Rome—albeit a short one—was a disaster. Unfulfilling. This was not the way she wanted to see Italy.

Lilly snorted after she remembered Marco's words.

This is no way to see Italy.

Okay, maybe he was right. Again. Not that he'd ever know since she would never see him again. She stopped walking and thought about it for a minute.

Would she see him again? She opened her purse, took

out his card, and read it.

"Marco Santini. General Manager. Santander Winery."

If you want to see Italy the right way, the way it was meant to be enjoyed and remembered and treasured, I would be happy to show you.

Maybe it was because of how frustrated she was or perhaps she was getting jet lag and wasn't thinking straight, but she was so tempted to call Marco.

So tempted.

Marco had a surprising amount of energy considering he flew over fifteen hours to get to Rome. Maybe he was motivated. As soon as he confirmed that everything was ready to go with their booth and sponsorship at the Lazio International Wine & Spirits Exhibition, he was free to do whatever he wanted for the next few days until he left for his trip next week to Australia.

He looked forward to traveling down south to Sorrento and seeing Stefano and Daniella. Other than that, everything else was up in the air and he would just take it day by day. The main thing was to relax and enjoy the moment.

He smiled, thinking of Lilly and her ridiculous itinerary. She had to be the most uptight woman he had ever met. He wondered how long she would last in Rome all by herself. She was too stubborn to even consider the possibility of him showing her around but he gave her the benefit of the doubt, anyway.

Truth be told, he would love to hear from her. It was always more fun sharing experiences with someone else. Yes, he'd been too busy working these last few years to have any fun at all, but now he had free time and wanted to take advantage of it.

With or without her, he would have fun.

Marco pulled the vibrating phone out of his pocket and eyed the caller ID. Someone from the US was calling but he didn't recognize the number.

"Go to voicemail or not go to voicemail?" he asked himself. "That is the question." He sighed and answered the call. "Hello?"

"Hi Marco. It's me, Lilly. We met on the plane."

Marco chuckled. "I don't think it's necessary to explain who you are. You told me all your deepest, darkest secrets while you were sleeping."

"Not funny."

"Okay, I'll laugh in private. How are you holding up so far with your touristy stuff?"

"Not so good."

"No? Can I help?" There was silence on the end of the phone call. "Lilly?"

"Maybe this is a bad idea."

"Well, if you are calling to ask me if I would help you rob a bank or pull off the biggest art gallery heist in the history of Italy, then you're right. Bad idea. But if it's something as simple as taking me up on my offer of showing you Italy the way it was meant to be seen, that's not a bad idea at all. All you have to do is ask." More silence. "Lilly?"

"Yeah. I...uh..." Lilly let out a deep breath into Marco's ear. "Please. Yes, please. I've had a horrible time since I've gotten here so if you would be so kind as to show me around, I'd appreciate it."

"It would be my pleasure, Lilly."

They made arrangements to meet in the morning around ten, after breakfast. Marco slipped the phone back into his pocket and smiled. He didn't know what they would do, but it didn't matter. He'd figure that out when he saw her. Then he would make sure she had the time of her life. He knew it wouldn't be easy though. A person as stubborn and set in her ways as Lilly was always a tough egg to crack.

Chapter Seven

The next morning Lilly went through her clothes, trying to decide what to wear that day. She didn't know what she and Marco would be doing, which made her nervous.

Her phone rang, and she checked the caller ID. It was Marco.

"You're here already?"

Marco laughed. "Yes. I'm in the lobby. You surprised I'm on time?"

"I guess I was hoping you'd be late. I'm just trying to figure out what to wear."

"It doesn't matter. Can you come down now?"

Lilly sighed. *Typical guy.* "As soon as I change. Tell me what we're going to do so I can plan my clothes accordingly."

"It's a surprise."

"I told you before. I don't do spontaneity."

"Well, then we need to break you out of that habit."

Now he was sounding like Colette. If this were another intervention she wouldn't have any part of it. It took all of her strength to get on the plane to Italy and too much change all at once would freak her out. She was certain she would end up hiding in her hotel room for the rest of the trip or trying to change her flight to head home early. She didn't need that pressure. She got plenty of that at home from Colette.

"Lilly Pilly?"

"Yes, Marco Polo."

"Quit thinking so much. Come downstairs. Trust me."

She shook her head. "Fine. I can't believe I'm going to do this but if something happens, you're one hundred percent to blame."

"I will take full responsibility."

"Darn right you will."

She disconnected and headed downstairs. As she got out of the elevator, she spotted Marco waiting by the reception area. Smiling.

Holy cow.

Was he that good-looking on the plane?

He wore dark blue jeans and a white short-sleeved shirt with the top two buttons undone. At least he didn't have a giant wad of hair coming out of the chest area. Did he have any hair at all?

"Are you looking at my chest?" he asked, kissing her on both cheeks. "Good to see you again."

Lilly felt her face heat up. "Good to see you too, and no, I wasn't looking at your chest." She thought about it for a moment. "Okay, maybe I was for a moment. It's just I've noticed that Italian men like to have a lot of buttons open and many of them have an unusually large amount of hair."

She looked around to make sure nobody heard her. "Well, not all of them. Maybe just the ones hitting on me."

Marco laughed. "An American woman in Italy. The men here will find you hard to resist. I'd like to tell you it'll be better now that you'll have a male companion but they don't care about that either. You will still get hit on."

"Great."

"But forget about that—let's go. Time for some fun."

"Okay, but just remember. I have a business meeting this afternoon at four. So whatever we do, we need to be back here before then."

"No problem."

Lilly followed Marco through the front doors of the hotel to the sidewalk. She wanted to know where they were going and it bugged the heck out of her. Maybe they should have planned this out. That's what any sensible person would have done. It's better to get all your ducks in a row so there's less chance of one of those ducks crapping all over you.

"Where are we going?" she asked.

He pointed across the street. "There."

She followed the direction of his pointing finger to the Colosseum. "What are you talking about? You know I already have plans to go there in a couple of days. I already paid for the ticket."

"Give away the ticket to someone."

Okay, this man was insane and needed to be locked up for a long time. There was no way she was going to the

Colosseum now and there was no way she would give away her ticket.

"You're thinking too much," he added.

"Thinking is good. And I've concluded that you are crazy. I'm going back to my room."

Marco laughed.

"Don't laugh at me. I'm serious."

"Why can't you go now?"

"Because it's wrong! And it wasn't planned! Besides, you can't get us in there. Most tickets are probably already sold out and those who don't have tickets have to wait in a line for a few hours just to get in."

Marco scratched his chin. "Tickets? You need tickets to get in there?"

"This was a mistake. Goodbye."

She turned to head back inside the hotel and Marco grabbed her arm. "I'm kidding. Sorry. The reason we don't need tickets is because I have a connection. I've already talked to him and he's expecting us."

"He's expecting us? What? In the back alley? Sounds pretty shady to me."

"First of all, the Colosseum doesn't have a back alley. Number two, you agreed to let me show you Italy the right way. At least give me one day for you to decide if it was worth it or not. Then, if you think you'd like to go back to your way, the wrong way, so be it. But I guarantee you that will not happen."

The man was so sure of himself she was wondering if it was all ego or if he knew what he was doing. Maybe she was the one with the ego. What if she found out he was right and all of that obsessive planning wasn't necessary? But he made a good point. Why not give him an opportunity to prove himself? He was a nice enough guy. Why not?

"Okay," Lilly answered. "One day. Show me what you've got."

Marco grinned. "It would be a pleasure. Take my hand."

She stared at his extended hand. "Why?"

"Once again. Trust me."

She stared at it again and then grabbed it. "Okay…"

"Stay close. Let's go."

They crossed the street, weaving in between cars, people, bicycles, and Vespas. It was a little scary but also exhilarating to watch him. He was so confident, and she liked that. He guided her toward the entrance of the Colosseum and then moved toward an unmarked ticket window. They were surrounded by hundreds and hundreds of people but Marco seemed unaffected by it all.

He leaned in and said something in Italian to the man in the booth. Nothing she recognized from her language program. The man opened a drawer, pulled out two tickets, and slid them to Marco under the glass.

"Perfect," he said to himself. "Okay, follow me."

Marco led her around the corner and she had to admit she enjoyed his take-charge attitude. She was surprised to find she enjoyed holding his hand. When was the last time she had held a man's hand? She couldn't even remember. It didn't matter, she enjoyed it.

She reeled her thoughts back to reality when she realized she was checking out his broad shoulders and firm butt.

Don't go there.

Marco was not on her list of potential future husbands. Yes, he was good-looking and yes, he was kind, but the man was going away for a long time. No way would she try a long-distance relationship. Marco was not an option. She would just enjoy her time with him and then keep an eye out for someone who was more suitable. Someone who didn't travel for work, for starters.

Marco led Lilly to an entrance different than the main entrance. There wasn't a line but there was an armed security guard. They emptied their pockets, placed their personal items in a tray and walked through the metal detector. Once they passed through, they grabbed their things and were waved over by another employee.

"I will take your tickets," he said.

Marco handed him the tickets, and the man asked them to follow him.

Marco turned to Lilly and grinned. "Let the fun begin."

Lilly didn't know what they would see and why this would be any different than what she had planned for Thursday, but she had to admit she felt a little excitement. It was like she had backstage passes to a sold-out concert and would meet the band.

They passed through a long hallway made of concrete—more like a tunnel—and came out on the other side into an open, covered area.

"Welcome to the underground," said the guide. "Please watch your step. As you can see, the Colosseum isn't perfect and much fell into disrepair from the severe damage sustained by lightning and earthquakes. But the most damage was caused by stone-robbers who took rocks and marble to use on other construction sites." He led them farther and pointed. "Many of the rooms and holding pens you see here once housed bloodthirsty gladiators and captive carnivores."

Lilly leaned into Marco. "It sounds kind of disgusting when he puts it that way."

Marco chuckled. "I agree. Hey, is that Russell Crowe?"

Lilly turned to look, then realized Marco was joking. She turned back toward him and held up her fist at the laughing man. "You want some of this?"

Marco stopped laughing and held up his palms. "No, no. You already showed me on the plane how much damage that thing can do. Put it away. I'll behave."

Lilly tried to keep a straight face. "You'd better."

They followed the tour guide around the corner until he pointed to some steps. "You're free to explore this area on your own. Please be careful."

She stared down at her sandals. "This is why I wanted to

know what we were going to do. Wearing sandals to climb these steps is not the brightest idea."

"You'll be fine," said Marco. "Just be careful."

Lilly walked up the steps with Marco trailing right behind her.

On the fourth step she banged her toes into the concrete. She screamed and fell backward right into the arms of Marco.

"I've got you," he said. "You smell fantastic."

She ground her teeth. "Let me go."

"Of course." He did as he was told. "You okay?"

"I'm not sure. I'll check the damage when we get to the top and there's more light."

"Can you walk on it? I can carry you to the top. It's not that far."

"Don't be ridiculous." She took another few steps and banged her foot in the same spot. She screamed and fell back into Marco's arms for the second time.

"Welcome back," he said. "Make yourself comfortable."

"That's it," she said. "Carry me up the rest of the way. And when we get there, put me down so I can kill you."

"That's premeditated murder."

"I told you I prefer to plan things. And why do you care? You'll be dead."

"Good point." He lifted her to get a better grip and carried Lilly a few more steps to the next level. He set her down and inspected her foot. It was a little red, but the skin didn't appear to be broken. He pointed to her foot. "No blood. That's a good sign."

"You are aware that you can break bones without breaking the skin?"

"Yeah, but—"

"I told you I don't do well with improvising and this proves it."

"No. This just proves you're clumsy and need to pay attention where you're walking."

"Excuse me?"

Lilly gave him a look, and he took a step back. Who did this guy think he was? It didn't matter he was right and she could have paid better attention to every step.

Marco pointed over toward the platform. "Look. That's safe there, and it has one of the best views. Let's just go over there and check it out. If you want to leave after that, no problem."

Lilly nodded. She was only a few feet away from the platform, so why not take a peek? Saying nothing else, she walked side by side with Marco to the edge. She looked out at the massive stone amphitheater, taking it in. It was as big as many of the sports and concert stadiums in the United States but made with tile, limestone, and concrete. It was difficult to comprehend how the Romans could build such a spectacular structure so long ago without all the modern day tools and machinery.

Marco turned to Lilly. "Amazing, isn't it?"

"Yes. I wonder what it was like to live in Rome two thousand years ago."

Marco frowned. "No Starbucks. No Netflix. No wonder they all wanted to kill each other."

Lilly burst in laughter. "You're crazy."

"And you're smiling. I need a picture of that." He pulled out his smart phone for a selfie of the two of them. "Perfect. Now we're going up to the third ring."

"What's that?"

"The third level where you will see one of the best views of ancient Rome."

Once up top they admired the sweeping views of the Colosseum interior and panoramic shot of the surrounding cityscape, Marco pulled out his phone for another selfie of the two of them. He checked the photo and showed Lilly. "See? Life isn't so bad."

"I never said it was bad. I said it was better when planned well."

"I will prove you wrong."

"Good luck."

They toured the Colosseum for another thirty minutes, entering a few more restricted areas thanks to Marco's connection. Lilly was fascinated with the Colosseum but had to admit she was more intrigued by Marco. Who was this guy and why was he growing on her?

"On to the next stop on the tour." Marco grabbed her hand and led her to the exit and she pulled him to a stop.

"That's it?" she asked. "We're inside the most visited tourist attraction in all of Italy, one of the most popular in Europe, and you want to leave already?"

He shrugged. "You saw something fascinating and historical. You even imagined what it must have been like to live in the era when this was in full use. Moving on! So, please follow me out and I'll take you around the corner for some wine tasting."

"It's not even lunchtime yet."

"Perfect. When we're done sampling the wine we'll look for a place to eat."

Lilly smirked. "I should have known you'd try to push the wine on me again."

"You've heard of the health benefits of wine?"

"I'm kidding. But I thought all the best wineries in Italy were in Tuscany."

"There are many wonderful wineries in Tuscany, but there are also some hidden gems right here in Lazio. We're not going to a winery though. I'm taking you to a wine room called Vino Roma. We'll sample the best of Italy in a wine cellar that's over a thousand years old." He held out his hand. "Trust me. You'll love it."

She stared at his hand. This was the problem. She *was* trusting him.

Chapter Eight

Marco was glad the wine tasting at Vino Roma went off with no issues. They had spent a couple of hours sampling wines from different regions in Italy, and chatted with the sommelier and a cute couple from Richmond, Virginia. They strolled down one of the busy streets of Rome and walking under the Arch of Constantine.

He glanced over at Lilly and grinned. "You look a little more relaxed."

Lilly smiled. "A lot more."

"You hungry?"

"Starving." Lilly pulled out her phone and scrolled. "Let's see our options."

Marco stopped. "What are you doing?"

"Searching for restaurants in the area. Then I can check out the reviews and—"

"Give me the phone."

"I'm not going to give you my phone."

"Yes, you are."

"No, I'm not."

"Yes, you are."

An older Italian man approached and shook his head.

Lilly waited for the man to pass before whispering, "No, Marco."

"You promised to give me a full day and do it my way, before concluding whether you enjoyed seeing Rome this way. Did you enjoy the wine tasting?"

"Yes, but—"

"Outside of the toe stubbing, did you enjoy the Colosseum?"

"Yes, but—"

"Then. Put. It. Away."

Lilly gave him a look and a moan before stuffing the phone back in her purse. "Fine. We only have about an hour and a half. Then I need to get back for a business meeting."

"Not a problem." Marco pointed to the quiet cobblestone street on the right. "This way."

They walked side by side, admiring the old buildings made of stone and the quaint shops and cafes.

Lilly stopped in front of a temple and stared at the front door. "Hang on a second."

Marco laughed. "It's been a while since your last confession?"

"Not funny. Wait here, okay?"

Marco studied her for a moment, wondering what she was up to. "No problem."

Lilly disappeared inside the temple and two minutes later came back out, frowning. "Okay, let's go."

Odd.

She obviously didn't want to talk about whatever was on her mind, so Marco didn't bring it up.

A few minutes later, Marco peeked inside the window of a restaurant, smiled, and gestured for Lilly to follow him. "Time to eat."

She peeked through the window as well and then glanced over to Marco. "How do we know if it's any good?"

"We don't. But there are people in there and nobody seems to be dying or dead, so that's a good sign."

Lilly reached for her phone again. "Let me just—"

Marco shook his finger at Lilly. "No, no. Come on."

He stepped inside and was greeted by an Italian woman who appeared to be in her fifties. She wore a beautiful white and red apron with images of pots and pans and utensils. The woman pointed to the table for two by the window.

"Grazie," said Marco, taking a seat.

Lilly stood in the doorway with her arms folded, tapping her foot on the floor.

He waved at the stubborn woman who finally sat. "That wasn't so difficult, was it?"

She picked up the napkin and inspected it. "Actually it was."

"You'll feel better after you eat."

They glanced around the restaurant and admired the dark wooden floors contrasted with elegant cream-colored tablecloths. It was a medium-sized place, around twenty tables. The people seemed to enjoy their food. One side of the restaurant had large mirrors on the wall, making the dining area appear larger.

"Nice place," said Marco, looking around.

"Not bad," said the stubborn woman across from him.

The server returned, smiled and placed bread and Chianti on the table.

Marco spoke with her in Italian about the food and turned to Lilly. "Do you like chicken, beef, seafood, or veggie?"

Lilly stared at him for a second. "Why?"

"It's a simple question. Do you like one of those or all of those?"

She hesitated for a moment and then answered. "Chicken."

Marco smiled at the woman. "Due pollo."

"Perfetto," said the woman, heading back to the kitchen.

Lilly watched the woman walk away and then turned to Marco. "What was that all about?"

He knew this would not go over well with Lilly but he had to tell her. She'd better not make a scene.

"Nothing, really," he answered. "It's just…they don't have menus here. Bread?" Marco broke off a piece of bread and chewed. "Hmm. This is good. You should try it."

Lilly's eyes wandered around the restaurant. "Wait, wait, wait. What do you mean they don't have menus? It's a restaurant. Restaurants have menus. "

Marco let out a nervous laugh. "Menus are not an

option. Pick either chicken, beef, seafood, or veggie. Then the chef will prepare his special of the day from that food group. I like that. It takes the difficulty of choosing something out of the equation."

"I like the difficulty of choosing something."

"This is not that type of restaurant. This place is Michelin-starred. No doubt they've got great food."

"This was a mistake. I should have stuck to the plan. I have things I want to see. Things I have to do." Lilly shook her head and popped a piece of bread in her mouth.

Marco smirked. "Things to do? You mean like...find a husband?"

Lilly choked and the piece of bread flew out of her mouth, smacking Marco in the chest.

<<<>>>

Lilly wiped her mouth and studied Marco. How did he know she was there to find a husband? It didn't make sense. The man knew no one she knew. They had never talked about it. She wasn't dumb enough to write it on her itinerary he saw during the layover in DC. Wait a minute...

The plane.

Sleep talking.

Crap.

"Marco," she said.

"Yes, Lilly Pilly?"

Rich Amooi

He could try to be cute but it wouldn't work with her. "Tell me everything you heard me say on the plane while I was sleeping."

He finished chewing another piece of bread and nodded. "Okay. Some of it made little sense but that shouldn't be a surprise because even when you're awake you sometimes don't make sense."

Lilly gave him a look that meant she was serious.

"Right. I know you like cappuccinos with two sugars."

"Go on…"

"You said something about a bear and an expensive car."

"Uh-huh…"

"Then something about a temple and finding your future husband in Italy." He took a sip of his Chianti. "You think spring weddings are lovely. I think they're lovely too." He winked and took another sip. "Oh. And you asked me to marry you."

The temperature of Lilly's face went from medium to hot. She took a big swig of her Chianti. Then she took another sip.

"Don't be embarrassed," said Marco. "Lots of people are looking for partners. Soulmates. I think it's kind of odd you thought you'd find him in Italy, though." He grinned. "Unless you've got a thing for Italians—hey, nothing wrong with that. We are a superior breed if I say so myself."

She stared at him, still unable to form words let alone sentences.

"I can help you find him," he continued. "Your future husband."

Lilly snorted. "Right." She took another sip of the Chianti and dismissed his ridiculous idea.

The woman returned with the two meals. "Due pollo. Buon appetito."

"Grazie," Marco said to the woman.

Can the man sound any sexier speaking Italian?

No wonder women fell for Italian men all the time.

Marco pulled his plate closer. "Why not let me help?"

"Not going to happen."

"Okay, think about it and let's eat."

"No."

"No to eating or no to helping?"

"No to you helping."

"It would be a pleasure to help you."

Lilly sighed. "Are we still talking about this?"

"Except for your crazy paranoia and obsession with planning, you're a total catch. I can tell you're sweet and caring. You're beautiful, there's no doubt there. Heck, if my life wasn't so messed up, I would be—" He shook his head. "Anyway, let's eat."

Heck, if my life wasn't so messed up, I would be...

Would be what? Why didn't he finish the sentence? Was he going to say he would be interested in Lilly if his life wasn't so messed up?

"Oh, wow," he said, after taking the first bite. "This is to die for. Please. Eat."

"I need it. I'm feeling a little tipsy."

Lilly looked down at her plate. It was a pasta dish with chicken, red bell peppers, and mushrooms. It looked and smelled amazing.

She took the first bite, God, it was good. She took another bite, this time chewing slower to savor the flavor. The portion wasn't big, so she needed to take her time with this meal or it would disappear too quickly. Another bite and she moaned.

She looked up and Marco had a satisfied smile on his face.

"Why are you smiling like that?" she asked, taking another bite.

"You look like you're enjoying the meal—that's all. I like to see that."

She finished chewing and nodded. "Okay, you were right. The food here is fantastic." She held out her glass of Chianti to toast. "To good meals and good times."

He clinked her glass. "Salud." He took a sip of his Chianti and grinned. "We can also toast to your future husband."

She set down her fork. "Are we back to that again?"

Marco laughed. "You shouldn't feel ashamed to talk about it. It's life. People want love and they should have it. You should have it."

"What about you?"

He shrugged.

"That's right," said Lilly. "Your life's so messed up."

"It is."

"Why is it messed up? You don't lack confidence, so what's missing?"

He took another sip of his Chianti.

This was where she was sure he would shut down, like most men did. Most didn't want to talk about their issues or feelings. Sometimes you had to choke it out of them but she wouldn't force the conversation. Marco was a good-looking man who appeared to be intelligent, so it was a surprise he wasn't married or at least seeing somebody.

He shrugged again and answered. "I don't have the life that warrants a relationship right now. I'm on the road all the time. I traveled over a hundred and fifty days last year. I don't expect to do it forever, but until that changes, it wouldn't be fair to whoever I'm with if I'm gone so long. It wouldn't be fun either."

"You're right. Doesn't sound like fun at all."

Marco glanced at her lips. "Life should be fun."

Her heartbeat sped up as she glanced at his lips. "Yeah. Fun is good."

Fun is good? What the hell am I doing? He saw me look at his lips! You're leading him on by doing something like that. Remember? He has a messed up life and won't be around for you. He's the last person you should be involved with. Knock it off!

"So, you're in the wine business…" said Lilly, hoping to

Rich Amooi

break the spell and change topics. "That sounds fascinating."

"It is," he said, pushing his empty plate forward on the table so he could use the place for his elbows. "But I think I'll be ready for a change soon."

"Doing what?"

"I'd like to make the wine myself."

Lilly sat up in her chair. "Like having your own winery?"

He nodded. "I know the business inside and out. When I'm not working on the road to promote our brand and expand the business, I'm at the winery working on promotions, marketing and managing the tasting room. I learned everything so I could step in at any moment, in any position, if help was needed or if we were short-staffed. What about you? Happy with your career?"

"Mostly, yes. I've got a lot of responsibilities, but I enjoy what I do."

"Which is?"

"Vice President of HR."

"Isn't that a boring job?"

"Hey."

Marco threw his palms in the air in defense. "Just asking!"

"Maybe it's not the most exciting job in the world. I get to work closely with people, which is nice. I used to work in sales many years ago and I enjoyed it much more, but it wasn't the most stable job in the world. So I switched careers."

"Why does the Vice President of HR come to Italy for work?"

Lilly didn't want to bore Marco to death, but the man seemed interested. "To convince a former employee who lives here now to come back and work with us. That's who I'm meeting for coffee at four o'clock."

Ten minutes later she ate the last bite of food on her plate and wiped her mouth. "One of the best meals ever."

"Good to hear it. I think the only thing you need now to make the day complete are a few sweet Italian kisses."

"Pardon me?" she said, glancing at his lips. Was he really suggesting such a thing?

"Don't tell me you've never tried them."

Lilly knew Marco had a lot confidence but for him to just come out and offer to kiss her caught her off guard.

"What do you say?" he continued. "Are you game? I may be a little biased but you are so missing out if you say no."

Lilly took the last sip of her Chianti and tried to clear her mind. Was he really talking about kissing her? Maybe she was just drunk and hallucinating. In fact, she didn't feel well. She hadn't kissed a man in over three years and just the thought of it was making her nervous and nauseated. She heard a gurgling sound in her lower belly.

What the heck was that?

The gurgle was followed by an abdominal cramp. All this was anxiety from a possible kiss? The pain was getting worse. She felt bloated. She needed to head to the bathroom.

"You okay?" asked Marco.

"I'm fine," she lied as a stronger cramp came on.

"Does this mean you'll pass on the dessert? If you don't like the regular Italian kisses, most likely they'll have mint chocolate."

Dessert? That's what he was talking about?

Lilly felt like an idiot. She also felt like she was going to throw up.

She stood as her stomach rumbled. "I need to use the ladies room."

"Of course." Marco stood up and pointed to the corner. "The women's bathroom is over there on the right side right."

She forced a smile and was already moving toward the bathroom. "Great. Be right back."

At least she hoped so. All of sudden it felt like she was going to die.

Chapter Nine

Yup. Lilly was dying.

That was the only logical reason to explain what was happening to her body at the moment. The cramps were pulling her intestines every which way but loose. The bloating was on a mission to test the maximum elasticity of her stomach. The nausea was encouraging the food she had eaten earlier to return to the stage for an encore performance.

Somebody please put me out of my misery.

On top of the pain was the embarrassment of knowing Marco was back at their table wondering what the hell happened to her for the last thirty minutes. Or had it been longer? She had lost complete track of time. In all the hurry, she'd left her purse hanging from her chair. She couldn't even check the time, but she knew she had to get out of there soon to go meet Roberto for coffee at four o'clock

Another giant rumble from her stomach told her maybe she wasn't close to finished there.

Lilly had been fine all day and even had a wonderful meal. She'd ruled out food poisoning since it was obvious the chicken was super fresh. Plus Marco had told her the restaurant was Michelin-starred, a supposed sign of quality.

Even the bathroom was clean—except for some writing on the back of the stall door. Most of it was written in Italian but there was one person who requested in English that Lilly call for a good time. Too bad she didn't have a pen or the energy to write down the phone number.

A good time sounds nice.

Another abdominal cramp came on, prompting her to latch onto both sides of the toilet seat and hold on for dear life. She could feel the pain start at the back near her kidneys, slowly build, rolling forward like an ocean wave, straight to her stomach.

"Ahhhh," she screamed, her voice echoing in the bathroom.

Her body wasn't done torturing her yet. Now she was sweating like an Italian pig. She didn't even want to imagine what it was doing to her makeup. She reached for the toilet paper to wipe her forehead and—

"No way."

There was exactly one square of paper left in the dispenser.

"No, no, no, no…"

She pulled off the square, removed the empty role, and stuck her hand up into the dispenser to feel around for another roll of toilet paper.

Zip.

She twisted around hoping to find a roll on top of the

water tank behind her.

Zilch.

She looked around the floor and to the other side.

Zero.

"This can't be happening."

With her skirt hiked up and her panties stretched from kneecap to kneecap like a ping pong net, Lilly opened the stall door and waddled toward the next stall like a drunk penguin. The sound of kids playing in the alley outside of the bathroom turned her attention toward the open window, but she blew it off. There were far more important things to worry about. She entered the other stall in search of precious toilet paper.

She reached down to the dispenser. "No way!"

No toilet paper there either.

Unbelievable.

There was only one thing she could do now. As uncomfortable as it would be, she needed to use paper towels to get the job done.

Lilly opened the stall door and made her way toward the sink, frowning. "You have *got* to be kidding me."

No paper towels.

Just an old-fashion electric hand dryer hung on the wall.

"Bingo," she said, perking up when she saw what was folded on top of the hand dryer. A newspaper with a picture of the Pope on the front page. She grabbed the newspaper and unfolded it, concluding that there would be plenty there to get the job done. "Better than nothing."

A loud knock at the door made Lilly jump. She stood motionless in the middle of the bathroom with her skirt still hiked up. Why did they knock? Three other women had entered earlier and none of them knocked, so it made little sense.

She searched her brain for the right word in Italian. "Ocupado." She wondered if that was Spanish, not Italian. "Occupato." Maybe they spoke English. "Occupied," she added for good measure.

"Lilly, you okay in there?"

Oh God.

Marco was just outside the bathroom. He wouldn't come in, would he?

More aliens invaded Lilly's body and were rearranging her inner organs but she needed to ignore the pain and say something, anything. "I'm okay."

She waited for a response, hoping he bought it.

"You don't sound okay."

Crap. Remain calm. "Go back to the table and relax. I'll be there shortly."

"If you say so."

"I say so."

At least the cramps had taken a breather. Now to the mission at hand, clean up.

"Bella!" said a young male voice behind her, so clear—as if he was in the bathroom with her. Lilly turned around and froze. Through the opening of the bathroom window she saw a phone pointed at her. Behind the phone was a smiling teenager.

She screamed and covered herself with the newspaper. The guy disappeared and a few seconds later there was another bang on the door.

"Lilly? What's going on in there?"

Marco again.

"Nothing! Just thought I saw a spider."

"I'll kill it for you. I'm coming in."

"No! Don't you dare. I'll be out in a moment."

He hesitated for a moment and then answered. "Okay…"

Lilly entered the stall again and locked the door. She sat back down on the toilet and prepared to use the newspaper to clean up. She stared at the Pope on the cover of the newspaper. "Cleanliness is holiness, right?" She carefully tore the Pope's head from the newspaper and placed it face down on top the toilet paper dispenser. "You don't want to see this."

Ten minutes later, Lilly stumbled out of the bathroom, a little low on energy, but cleaned up and feeling better. She was worried about the time. How long had she been in there?

She passed the kitchen and glanced at the chef preparing a pasta dish, smiling, adding cream to the pan. She stopped and bit the inside of her lip. "Cream. Lactose."

Lilly was lactose intolerant.

Whatever she had eaten had cream in it. That had to be it.

She couldn't believe she didn't figure it out sooner. She continued to their table and Marco stood, a worried look on his face. He rubbed Lilly's shoulder. "You sure you're okay? You were in there forever. You look pale." He pulled out her chair. "Please sit down."

"We should go. Plus, I need to get some fresh air."

"I'll take care of the bill if you'd like to wait for me outside. I'll be right there."

"Thank you. I appreciate it." Lilly grabbed her purse hanging from the chair and waved to the woman. "Grazie."

Lilly went outside and stopped near the front window. The deep breath of fresh air she took in was a combination of relief and happiness entering her lungs, traveling to her insides that were ripped apart by Hurricane Lactose. If that episode in the bathroom was anything like having a baby, she would adopt.

Marco came out of the restaurant and closed the door behind him. "At first I thought maybe you tried to crawl out of the window and ditch me. But after we heard screams coming from the bathroom, I knew something was wrong."

"Something wrong would be an understatement," she said, feeling fifty pounds lighter. "There must have been cream or cheese in that meal. I'm lactose intolerant."

"Oh God. Why didn't you mention that earlier when we

arrived?"

She shrugged, wondering the same thing. "I wanted to believe you when you said it was good to be spontaneous. I've missed doing things in the spur of the moment and wanted to try it again. Look where it got me."

She contemplated telling Marco about the peeping Tomasso in the bathroom but decided against it. She'd had enough humiliation for one day.

Marco turned to her, a sincere look on his face. Or maybe it was guilt. "Sorry."

"Don't worry about it. Lactose happens." She pulled her cell phone from her purse to check the time and saw two missed calls and two voicemails. "Just a second. I need to check this." Lilly tapped the voicemail button.

"Hi, Lilly. It's Roberto. Not sure where you are but hopefully you're on your way. I can only wait for about another twenty minutes and then I will have to take off. I'm traveling south to visit family in Capri and Positano. Okay... hope to see you soon."

Lilly stared at her phone. "I don't understand..."

"What?" asked Marco.

"Just a second." She listened to the second voicemail.

"Lilly, it's Janet. I was hoping to hear from you by now. I hope that's not a bad sign. Let me know what's happening with Roberto. We need him to come back to work for us, so do whatever you need to, to make it happen. Keep updated."

Lilly slid the phone back into her purse. "How long was I in the bathroom?"

Marco shrugged. "I lost track of time...maybe forty-five minutes."

Lilly jerked her head back. "Oh God. We need to go. Now!"

"Where?"

"Back to my hotel. I was supposed to meet Roberto a half hour ago. The future of my company could on the line. What's the fastest way to get there?"

"The train. Can you run to the station with your stubbed toes?"

"I guess I have no other option."

Lilly followed Marco down the cobblestone street to the end and they turned down the main artery of the city. Five minutes later they passed through the turnstiles of the train station and were heading toward her hotel on the train. Out of breath.

She tried returning Roberto's call but there was no signal underground on the train.

"This is bad," she said, sighing. "Really bad."

"Don't worry. Everything will be okay."

Lilly wasn't so optimistic. She had a bad feeling about this.

Ten minutes later they exited the train at the Colosseum exit and crossed the street, entering the hotel and running straight back to the cafe.

Out of breath and feeling weak, she scanned the cafe for Roberto.

Marco stepped forward, also looking around. "Do you see him?"

Lilly shook her head. "I don't think he's here."

"Try calling him again."

Good idea. She pulled her phone out and dialed Roberto's number. "Straight to voicemail again." She felt the pulse in her neck and temples, letting her know that she was screwed. She turned to Marco and gave him a look to make sure he knew just how unhappy she was.

It was his fault. If she would have stuck with her plan, none of this would have happened.

"Why are you looking at me that way?" Marco asked. "You're scaring me a little."

She took a step toward Marco. "Roberto is on his way to Capri."

"Oh…"

"We're late because of you," she said, poking him in the chest. "You need to fix this."

"I'm sorry—I really am, but what can I do now?"

"*You* need to help me find Roberto. We're going to Capri."

Chapter Ten

The next morning, Lilly grabbed her carryon and made her way down to the lobby of the hotel. She was headed to the island of Capri with Marco. She needed to talk with Roberto and get him to sign the contract, but she couldn't believe she was going to do this with Marco. Not a surprise she barely slept at all last night. Why was she nervous? They were going to find Roberto, not go away for a romantic weekend.

This was strictly business.

Still, she couldn't overlook that Marco was a good-looking and kind and fun. What did that have to do with anything?

Business.

Marco probably thought Lilly was being spontaneous, but she had spent two hours doing research about Capri on the hotel's business center computer.

She entered the lobby and spotted Marco waiting by the entrance.

He smiled and approached her. "Good morning, Lilly Pilly."

She smirked. "Good morning, Marco Polo."

He chuckled and kissed her on both cheeks. "You look

great."

"No compliments. This is business, nothing more."

He placed his hand on his chest. "Wow. Where did that come from?"

"Never mind. What's the plan?"

She had been wondering all morning what he would come up with. She was ready to let him know right then and there and they were not going to improvise, but first she wanted to hear what he had to say.

Marco smiled. "I'm so glad you asked! We're taking the train to Naples. From there, we take the ferry to Capri. And if it makes you feel any better, I bought the train and ferry tickets in advance. I planned ahead!"

"I'm impressed. Then what?"

"Not a clue."

Lilly sighed and pulled a piece of paper out of her purse. "I had a feeling you would say that, so I did a little research last night and printed this out in the hotel's business center."

He stared at the paper. "Let me see."

She handed him the paper, and he analyzed it. "This has got to go." He moved like he was going to tear it into pieces.

"Give me that." She grabbed it back out of his hand. She needed to protect that document and at least keep it as a backup plan. Better safe than sorry. She folded it and slid it back into her purse. "Okay, let's go. And behave."

Lilly gave him a playful swat on the hand.

Marco grinned. "Behave is my middle name. Anyway, I

was kidding about not having a clue. It shouldn't be too difficult to find Roberto's family's home. Capri is tiny and is mostly populated with tourists. All the locals know each other, so all we have to do is ask one of them. Should be easy. What's Roberto's last name?"

"Rossi."

Marco laughed. "Okay, maybe it will take a little work, considering he has one of the most popular names in all of Italy. We'll find him—don't worry. We'll also find you a husband."

She raised an eyebrow at him, not amused he was teasing her. "You want me to wipe that grin off your face?"

He laughed again. "I'll do it." He waved his hand over his face like a magic wand. His smile disappeared. "There. Done."

Twenty minutes later they were on a train traveling south toward Naples, admiring the Italian countryside and the lesser-known cities like Monte San Biagio and Cicerone.

Marco gestured toward the front of the train. "Looks like you have a fan. Potential husband?"

Lilly glanced toward the kid who was smiling at her. "You trying to get me in jail? He looks like he's twelve."

"He's at least eighteen, I guarantee it."

"You can add another ten years to that and he'll still be too young. I prefer to meet someone around thirty."

"Like me," Marco said, sitting up straight and grinning.

"You're thirty?"

He nodded. "Exactly thirty to the day."

Lilly blinked. "Today's your birthday?"

He nodded again.

"How come you didn't say anything?"

"I just did."

"No. I mean, earlier. Or yesterday. And why are you spending your birthday with a stranger on a train? Don't you want to be with family or friends?"

He twisted his body so he could face her a little better. "I don't go around advertising my birthday. And why am I spending my birthday with a stranger? First, I don't consider you a stranger anymore. You gave up your stranger status on the plane when you asked me to marry you."

"I was asleep. That doesn't count."

"Does too." Marco laughed. "It's amazing what I learned about you while you slept."

"Tell me what you know about me that doesn't have to do with being a teeny bit uptight about planning or my body's hatred of lactose. You've got nothing."

Most men were clueless about women. Marco didn't know her. What could he know about her? She tucked her hair behind her ears and waited for him to respond.

"There." He pointed to her head. "Right there."

"Right where?"

"That thing you do with your hair."

"What *thing*?"

"You always tuck hair behind your ears when you get

nervous or uncomfortable."

She raised her hand to tuck her hair behind her ears again and dropped it back down to her lap. "I do not."

He was right. That's amazing. She didn't even know she did that. It was subconscious, but he was right. How did he notice subtle nuances like that? Nobody else had ever mentioned that before, but wow… She placed one hand over the other, trying to hold it down. His intense, confident gaze stayed with her and she needed to say something.

"Okay." She tried to think of something else. "You got lucky. Maybe I do that occasionally."

Marco chuckled. "Or all the time."

She tucked her hair behind her ears. "Let's change the subject."

"You did it again."

"Crap!"

They arrived in Naples an hour later. It was a beautiful day, and the streets were crowded with locals and tourists.

Marco pointed. "This way… Before we catch the ferry you're going to enjoy the best pizza in the world."

Lilly stopped. "The cheese. Remember?"

"I remember. This pizza is so good it doesn't need cheese."

"That's the most ridiculous thing I've ever heard. Cheese makes the pizza."

"Yeah? Not in Italy. You just wait."

They continued their walk and approached three

teenage kids leaning against the wall, all on their phones. One of them looked up and pointed at Lilly, saying something in Italian. The other two looked up, one of them appearing to be surprised. They said something else in Italian and Marco laughed.

Lilly glanced back at them. "What did they say?"

"Something about you and the Pope in the bathroom."

Lilly stopped.

Marco continued on ahead of her and then stopped, turning back around. "What?"

She didn't answer and moved toward him, trying to piece everything together.

A teenage boy smiled at Lilly, then showed his grandmother something on his phone. The woman eyed the phone, gasped, and then looked up at Lilly. She moved in Lilly's direction, rolled up her newspaper, and swatted Lilly on the arm with it.

Marco watched the woman walk away and then turned to Lilly. "Are you an escaped convict or something? These people know you?"

She was sure she knew what was going on and was horrified at the thought. How could this happen? She flashed back to her time in the bathroom and what she went through. The pain. The lack of toilet paper. The newspaper with the picture of the Pope. And the biggest shock of them all, the kid who took her picture through the open window.

Another person approached and snapped a picture of

Lilly.

Lilly moved faster down the sidewalk. "I could just die. Get a move on." They continued down the street until Lilly spotted an alley to hide.

Marco followed and then looked back to the street. "What's going on?"

"I think I went viral."

Marco felt bad but he couldn't stop laughing. How in the world did Lilly go from being so sick in an Italian restaurant to becoming an Internet star? He stopped another teenager who took Lilly's picture. The kid showed Marco a photo of Lilly in the bathroom in a compromising position.

"Quit laughing," said Lilly. "This is not funny. How am I going to walk the streets or be anywhere in public? This is your fault."

Marco placed his hand on his chest. "My fault? How is this my fault?"

"You were the one who wanted to go to that restaurant. A restaurant without menus for a person who is lactose intolerant is like walking into a minefield."

"You could have told me you were lactose intolerant when I mentioned there were no menus. That should have been the first thing out of your mouth. And besides that, what were you doing walking around the bathroom half naked with a picture of the Pope?"

Lilly explained what happened and Marco laughed again.

"I'm going back to Rome," said Lilly, turning to leave the alley.

"Oh no you're not," said Marco. "I'm sorry." A large group of teenagers approached, all with smart phones in their hands. "Come here." Marco grabbed Lilly's carryon and rolled it with his toward the bakery behind them. "Quick. Hug me."

"I'm not going to—"

Marco yanked her in his direction and wrapped his arms around her.

"Relax," whispered Marco. "There's a large group of kids coming this way. I'm just hiding you, that's all."

Marco hoped the kids took their time because he enjoyed having Lilly in his arms. When was the last time he was this close to a woman? So sad that he couldn't even remember. He missed it so much.

Maybe he could milk it a little longer. "I'll let you know when they pass."

Lilly didn't seem to mind at all. A few seconds later, she relaxed and moved her face to the side of his neck. Holy cow, she smelled amazing.

"Are you sniffing me?" Lilly asked.

"Maybe…"

Lilly laughed. "You're not sure?"

"Okay, I am. I can't help it—you smell great."

Lilly cleared her throat. "I don't hear the kids anymore."

Marco pulled away and looked into her eyes. "Yeah…"

Damn, she was gorgeous.

She looked away and tucked a few strands of hair behind her ear. They had a nice little intimate moment there, but he wasn't going to mention a thing.

Lilly shook her head like she was trying to remember something. "What were we talking about before the teenagers walked by?"

"You were being a big baby, saying you were going back to Rome."

"Big baby? Come on. I don't want to spend the entire trip being laughed at by the citizens of Italy. Better to hide in my hotel room."

"No way. I've got a quick fix for this and then we can go to have the pizza."

Lilly studied Marco for a moment. "You can fix this?"

"Absolutely," he answered with all the confidence in the world. "I have an idea,"

"You always have ideas—that's the problem."

"Trust me." He grabbed her by the hand. "Follow me and keep your head down."

Lilly sighed. "Why not? It can't get much worse, can it?"

Marco didn't answer. He led Lilly down the street a few blocks and made a right and then the first left. A few minutes later Marco found what he was looking for and stopped. "Here."

Lilly stared at the giant sign on the glass door. "Parrucchiere."

He nodded. "Superb pronunciation."

"Thank you, but what is this place?"

"Take a peek inside."

Lilly put her hand against the glass to block the glare so she could see the inside of the business. "I see glass shelves filled from top to bottom with fancy bottles of shampoo, conditioner, mouse, gel, and other hair products. And three salon chairs. All empty. You're suddenly in the mood for haircut?"

He grinned. "No, but you are."

She did a double take. "What? Me?" She let out a nervous laugh. "No way."

"This is the perfect way for you to take on a different appearance, so people won't connect you with the Pope."

"No. I would feel like I'm in the witness protection program."

"When was the last time you did something different with your hair?"

"Never."

"Never?"

Lilly shook her head. "Never."

Marco stared at her for a moment, confused. "You're a woman, right?"

"I don't like change, remember?"

"I thought you didn't like to do things if they weren't planned. Have you ever wanted to try something different with your hair?"

"They could make a huge mistake and have to chop it all off."

"Yes or no. Have you ever wanted to try something different with your hair?"

She looked deep in thought. "Yes. I've always wanted to have it darker. Black."

"I think you'd look amazing with black hair." Marco swung open the door. "This won't take long and then you won't have to worry about people harassing you or wanting to take their picture with you."

Lilly just stood there.

Marco pointed to her feet. "See those things attached to the bottom of your legs? They're called feet. Use them!"

Lilly stared at the open door as Marco contemplated dragging her inside.

Chapter Eleven

Two hours later, Gino the stylist spun Lilly around in the salon chair until she faced the mirror.

"Another masterpiece!" he said with his thick Italian accent. A proud smile formed on his face. "You are like sweet chocolate for my eyes."

"Grazie." Lilly turned her head to the left, then to the right, admiring her new look. She had to admit, she was rocking it. She loved it so much she wanted to scream.

This was a huge breakthrough.

She couldn't remember the last time she had done something so drastic, so out of character.

So spontaneous.

She felt exhilarated and alive.

Marco set the magazine on the table and stood. He had promised not to look until her hair was done. He took a few steps toward her and stopped. She loved the way he was looking at her. She felt like a rock star. Like a diva.

Like *some*body.

He took another few steps toward her and nodded his approval. "I didn't think you could get any more beautiful. I was so wrong."

Gino removed the cape from around Lilly and she stood, thinking about what Marco had said.

Was he aware that that was exactly what she needed to hear? Was he aware that she wanted to kiss him right there at that moment?

Marco's gaze dropped to her lips.

Yup. I think he's very aware of what's going through my mind.

But as tempting as his lips were, she wouldn't be kissing them. They didn't have a future together. The more time she spent with him the more she liked him, but that was it. It would never go from like to love. Still, there was nothing wrong with thanking him for this breakthrough.

She stepped forward and kissed him on the cheek. "Thank you. I owe this all to you."

"I did nothing. You were the one who did this." He continued to stare at her lips. He needed to stop doing that.

"I think you forced me to come in here. Maybe even threatened me."

Marco laughed and pulled out his wallet, flipping through the bills.

"Put that away," Lilly said. There was no way she would let Marco pay for her new hairdo. He'd already paid for the meal yesterday, plus the train tickets. And it was his birthday!

Before she could pull her wallet out of her purse, Marco already had handed the money to Gino. "Grazie." He turned to Lilly. "Too late. Sorry about that."

She pushed her wallet back into her purse and zipped it

closed. "Right. You look *so* sorry."

Marco laughed and pointed to the door. "If it makes you feel any better, you can treat me to pizza."

She thanked Gino, grabbed the handle of her suitcase and rolled it outside, following Marco. "That's right. The famous pizzeria with the cheese-less pizza. This I gotta see."

"It's not just pizza they're famous for," said Marco, leading her down the sidewalk.

"What else do they offer? Cheese-less cheese puffs? A cheese-less grilled cheese sandwich? How about a—"

"Okay, you just wait and see."

Lilly laughed and thought about the pizza. When was the last time she had one? The truth was she missed eating it and a cheese-less pizza would be amazing, if it was just as enjoyable. She didn't see how it would be possible to pull off such a feat.

A few minutes later Marco pointed across the street at the long line of people on the sidewalk.

"Are we going to wait in that line?"

"It goes faster than you think."

They crossed the street and passed all the people, stopping right in front of the entrance.

"I'll be right back," said Marco, rolling his suitcase alongside Lilly's. "I need to grab a ticket with a number."

"Okay," said Lilly, placing her free hand on the handle of Marco's carryon. Any doubts of this being a good pizza place were erased from her brain after seeing the wait.

She glanced up at the sign. "Pizzeria da Michele."

The name sounded familiar. She'd never been to Naples before, so it made little sense. The building looked familiar too. And the inside. Maybe she was having a déjà vu moment.

Weird.

Marco came back out and waved the ticket at Lilly. "Got it." He studied Lilly for a second and frowned. "Why do you look so confused?"

"It's just...I almost feel as if I've been here before. There's something so familiar..."

Marco laughed. "A past life?"

"I don't think so."

"Well, you'll be happy to know they have menus here."

She eyed the menu on the wall, noticing the world's smallest menu. "They only have two types of pizzas?"

He grinned. "Margarita and marinara. One with cheese. One without."

"Huh..."

"I want to sit where Julia Roberts sat," said a female voice behind Lilly.

Lilly turned to look at the woman and then read the sign on the building again. "Pizzeria da Michele."

"Practicing your Italian?" Marco asked. "Excellent."

"Hang on," said Lilly, trying to focus. "This is the pizzeria from *Eat, Pray, Love.*"

"I told you they were famous for more than just their

pizza napolitana."

She looked inside and spotted a picture of Julia Roberts on the wall. Lilly had read *Eat, Pray, Love* and had seen the movie twice.

An hour later their number was called and Marco and Lilly both ordered marinara pizzas with beer.

She wondered if Marco had ordered the cheese-less pizza because of her, but didn't ask.

Once they could grab an open table they sat, and Lilly held out her beer bottle. "Happy birthday."

Marco clinked her bottle. "Thank you."

The pizza was chewy and tasty and it had no cheese! How was that possible?

After Lilly's third delicious bite, she set the slice down when she noticed something odd.

Marco's pizza sat there uneaten, his eyes intense on Lilly. He took a sip of his beer and smiled.

What are you waiting for?

She took another bite, enjoying the amazing flavor, but she was feeling self-conscious. He was the one who convinced her that this was the best pizza ever, and he wasn't even touching it.

"Okay, knock it off and eat your pizza," she said.

"You still haven't said how much you like the pizza."

"My moaning didn't give you a clue?"

"I need to hear from your lips."

"Fine. My lips will tell you that this is incredible pizza,

and you were right."

"I'm always right."

Lilly smirked. "And humble." She looked around the pizzeria and smiled. "I can't believe I'm here. I love being in places where they've shot movies. I'm a big Elizabeth Gilbert fan too and I'm going to see her next week."

"Socializing with the elite? What are you doing with Elizabeth Gilbert? Champagne brunch? Pajama sleepover?"

Lilly laughed. "Not quite. She's giving a lecture in Berkeley and my best friend and I have tickets. I'm *so* looking forward to it." She glanced around the place again. "This was a wonderful surprise coming here. Thank you for bringing me."

"My pleasure." He took another sip of his beer before taking his first bite of pizza. "I'm enjoying this very much."

She smiled, feeling very relaxed. "Me too. No cheese. Who would have thought it?"

He was about to take another bite of his pizza and stopped. "No, no. I mean you. I'm very much enjoying your company."

"Oh…"

His gaze dropped to her mouth.

She took a deep breath and then took a swig of her beer. She had visions of her lips stuck on his instead of the beer bottle and that wasn't good.

He took a bite of the pizza and smiled.

That smile would be the death of her.

<<<>>>

Marco had to use all his strength not to stare at Lilly. He couldn't help it. She was already a knockout before the new hair but now she was a double knockout. Triple even.

But it was more than the hair. Lilly had much more confidence and that was such a turn-on. Funny how that happened. He wanted her to relax, to not be recognized. She got much more than that.

Lilly wiped her mouth. "Do I have pizza sauce on my face?"

"No," said Marco, catching himself looking at her lips again. "All clean."

"Then why are you staring at me?"

God. Idiot. "Sorry… I like your new hair. It suits you." *And I also want to kiss you so badly.*

"Oh… Thank you."

"Thank *you*."

Thank you? What the hell was that?

He knew exactly what it was. The stupidest thing ever.

They finished their pizza and beers, took a selfie out front, and then squeezed through the crowd on their way to the ferry. They would take the high-speed catamaran which would get them to the island of Capri in less than an hour.

After boarding the vessel, Marco and Lilly made their way to the front and grabbed a seat with an unobstructed view of the water. A few minutes later they were off and flying across the water.

Lilly closed her eyes and inhaled a deep breath of the fresh Mediterranean air.

Marco watched her, admiring her nose and mouth and chin. Especially her mouth.

She opened her eyes and turned to him. "This is wonderful. Thank you. I was missing something and I think I've found it."

"What were you missing?"

The look on her face was sincere. "Life. This will sound hokey—but I'm seeing things a little clearer again."

"That's not hokey at all. I haven't had much of a life lately. It's been all work and moments like these are needed, although I'd prefer they happened more often. Or all the time."

She closed her eyes again and took another deep breath. "Yeah."

"What happened to you?" God, there he was, sticking his foot in his mouth again. He was distracted by her luscious lips again. "Sorry. You don't have to answer that."

She patted the top of his leg. "It's okay, I don't mind..." His gaze traveled down to her hand that was touching him, but she removed it. "I admit I've got some baggage. I was eight when my dad left us. Me and my mom. He said he needed to get away and forget about life for a while. Said he'd be back soon. He ended up in Miami, Florida. No suitcase, no plan. He took a taxi to the airport and got on the next flight, totally spur of the moment." She looked to the Mediterranean and shrugged. "You can guess where this is going. He never returned. Never heard from him again."

Marco grabbed her hand and squeezed it. "I'm sorry you had to go through that. It had to be very difficult."

"The worst. I thought I had gotten past it but when my boyfriend did the same thing a few years ago, I went through a rough patch. I retreated into my safe haven. I stopped going out. Stopped dating. Stopped having fun. I know it's not the healthiest thing to do but…"

"We all cope with hardships in different ways."

"Yeah…" She nodded and turned to Marco. "I can't believe I told you that story. And you've helped me. Don't tell me you haven't, because you have."

He didn't know how to respond. *My pleasure* was all he could come up with. The truth was he wanted to help, enjoyed helping, felt great helping. What could be better than helping another person have a good time without the fear of the consequences? He squeezed her hand again and smiled. She returned the smile and then dropped her gaze to his lips.

Please don't do that because it makes me want to kiss you.

Marco didn't have to worry about being presumptuous and making a move because Lilly leaned toward him and kissed him. She held her lips against his for a few magical moments and then pulled away, keeping eye contact with him. "Oh…I…"

Marco's pulse sped up. There was no doubt in his mind he wanted more of that. Before she could utter another word, he pressed his lips back together with hers. He pulled her closer and deepened the kiss. The Mediterranean breeze blowing through his hair and the warm sun on his back heightened the experience, and he didn't want the kiss to end.

But it did.

Lilly pulled away and touched her lips with her fingertips. "I don't understand what just happened there."

"It's called kissing. Lots of people seem to do it these days."

"First, we were talking and next thing I knew you were kissing me."

Marco chuckled and shook his head. "I recall it a tad bit differently. We were talking and next thing I knew *you* were kissing *me*."

"Still. How did that happen?"

"That's life…things just happen. Naturally." He grinned and leaned in. "But if you really want to get to the bottom of it, we could do it again and then carefully analyze every moment."

Lilly placed her palm on his chest, pushing him away. "I'm serious."

"So am I. Didn't you enjoy the kiss?"

"I think it was obvious I did, and that's what scares me."

She stood and took a deep breath. "What are we doing?"

Marco stood and moved closer. "Enjoying each other's company."

"You're going to Australia for months, so how can this go anywhere?"

Sometimes it takes hours or days for men to figure out what was on a woman's mind, so this was a new concept for Marco. She just came out and said it.

Hallelujah!

But she made a good point. He was attracted to Lilly, mentally and physically, but what happened at the end of the week when he had to go? It wasn't like he wouldn't go to Australia.

"Not a good sign when you're so quiet," she said.

"I was thinking. I don't know...I've never been in this position before. Here's the deal if it's not obvious by now. I'm attracted to you, Lilly. A lot. And I want to spend as much time with you as possible before I go. Can't we have a good time and enjoy the moment?"

Lilly looked surprised by his honesty. Marco wasn't sure if that was a good thing or a bad thing. She nodded and seemed to consider his suggestion.

Don't say no. Don't say no. Don't say no.

"I don't think that's such a good idea."

Wrong answer!

But Marco wouldn't give up that easy. "Well, we have a few more minutes until we get to Capri. I guess I'd better use

119

that time wisely to convince you why it's a *great* idea."

He grinned and then leaned in, kissing her again.

Chapter Twelve

Lilly couldn't remember the last time she enjoyed a kiss like that. She loved the way Marco took control and pulled her closer with so much passion. It was wonderful being in his arms and kissing him. Too bad her stupid, sensible brain got involved and let her know that kissing Marco was just plain dumb and wrong. This was what she had been avoiding the last few years so she couldn't be hurt again. Where was her heart when she needed it?

She wondered what was going through Marco's mind. He didn't look too worried. That was one of the other things she liked about him. His confidence. She sat and waited for him to say something.

"Lilly," he said, taking a seat next to her and grinning. "Just a friendly warning that I'll kiss you again in about one minute."

Lilly laughed. "That sounded like the pre-boarding announcement at the airport. Nice try. You're still not going to kiss me."

"You're right. I've changed my mind."

"Good," she said, not meaning it at all. "We need to focus on finding Roberto."

They approached the dock in Capri and Marco pointed to a dramatic rock formation in the middle of the water just off the coast. "See that?"

She nodded, not having a clue what it was. "Yes. Rocks."

Marco chuckled. "Not just any rocks. It's called the Faraglioni."

Lilly stood to get a better look. "It's amazing."

"It's Capri's most iconic sight. The Faraglioni rock formations tower an average of three hundred feet above the surface of the sea. Seeing it up close is a must for anybody who comes to the south of Italy."

"A must…" Lilly said.

"That's why I want to take you out there."

She turned to Marco and stared at him, then turned her attention back out to the rocks. "What exactly do you mean, take me out there?"

"I'm glad you asked. I will hire a skipper to sail toward the Faraglioni. We'll sail right through the stone archway of the second stack which is called Faraglione di Mezzo. Once we are underneath you'll kiss me."

Lilly snorted. "I will kiss you?"

"Yes."

"And why would I do that?"

"One, because it's enjoyable. And two, it's good luck."

"I'm sure you made that up so you can get another a kiss."

"I assure you it's the truth."

"Why is it good luck?"

Marco shrugged. "I have no clue. It's just always been good luck. Why is a four-leaf clover good luck? Or a rabbit's foot? But why not believe? Look, how about if we go out there and then we go find Roberto? Or you can go back to Rome if you're a chicken. Deal?" She gave him a look. "Okay, I see you look a little skeptical."

"Not a little. A lot. You're up to something." She pointed to his face. "Tell me the truth."

He tried to give her his best Jack Nicholson. "You can't handle the truth."

She laughed and followed Marco off the ferry. They made their way toward the other side of the harbor and Marco stopped in front of the boat tours office.

"We don't have time for this," Lilly said. "We need to find Roberto."

"Finding Roberto won't take long at all. We have all night for that." He pointed out to the Faraglioni. "But the boats will stop going out *there* in couple of hours. Let's just go for a quick sail and we'll be back before you know it. Then we'll find Roberto."

Lilly stared at the boat tour sign written in Italian and English. "Is this safe?"

"This is a good question. Just the fact you asked me that question tells me you're considering going with me. Let me ask you this. When do you think you will have time to come back to Italy?"

"Maybe never."

Marco chuckled and placed his hand on her shoulder. "Okay, I don't believe that. You'll miss this place when you go home. I'm sure of it. And you have to return to explore Florence and Venice and Verona, and the other beautiful places north of Rome. I haven't been through what you've been through, but still... Are you sure you want to deny yourself the pleasure of something so wonderful? I'm talking about the kiss and not the rocks." He laughed and stepped back out of reach when Lilly tried to smack him on the arm.

"Fine," she said, shaking her head. "I'll go."

"Great!"

She followed him down a few steps to the boat rental office. "If you ever give up wine, you would be a great salesman selling kitchen gadgets late at night on television. Or maybe a hostage negotiator. I can't say no to you."

"Then it looks like we'll get along just fine."

It was a beautiful day on the water. The Mediterranean was sparkling from the sun. Marco sat in the back of the boat with Lilly to his side as they sailed toward Faraglione di Mezzo. The closer they got, the faster his heart beat. He was so excited to share with her the wonders of Faraglione but another kiss from her was his predominant thought. He glanced over and her attention was on the water, watching as they approached the rocks.

Lilly stretched her legs out in front of her on the padded bench and took in the bright sun and the warm sea breeze. Marco loved that look on her face. Something about it said she was relaxed. Satisfied. Not a care in the world. She was the girl Marco could easily fall for, even with all of her quirks and flaws. That's what made her unique and amazing. Hell, he had plenty of flaws himself.

"Almost there," he said, stating the obvious. Lilly had been silent since they left the dock and he was curious what was on her mind.

"I hope you don't think you're getting a kiss," she said. "Not going to happen."

"You're thinking too much—knock it off. Relax and enjoy this, would ya?"

"Fine," she said, getting her attention back on the water and Faraglione di Mezzo. "You're still not getting a kiss."

"We'll see about that."

Dominic the skipper maneuvered the boat around the first stack and approached Faraglione di Mezzo. He slowed the boat down and then killed the engine once they were underneath the rock. The small waves crashed against the rock and the boat rocked gently back and forth.

"Well?" said Marco, curious of what she thought. She had to be impressed with such a beautiful creation from Mother Nature.

Lilly scooted along the bench seat, closer to Marco and

then stood up underneath the archway. "No kiss."

Marco shrugged. "Fine. Your loss."

"My loss?"

"Of course."

"Right. You mean *your* loss."

He thought about it. "Okay, I admit it. It's my loss."

She squished her eyebrows together, most certainly confused by what he had said. Good. It was all a set-up, and he just waited it out.

She chuckled, admiring the inside of the archway. "How long are we going to stay under here?"

"In a hurry?"

"No, no. It's amazing."

"Well, if you must know, I gave specific instructions to Dominic to stay here. Until you kiss me."

Lilly glanced over to Dominic who smiled and nodded. "It's true. He offered me a big tip."

She huffed and folded her arms. "Then I guess we'll be here a long time."

"If that's how you want to play, then sure. I've got patience. Just the thought of kissing you again will keep me going for hours." He took a seat, leaned back and clasped his hands behind his head, taking in the breathtaking sight before him. Lilly in front of the rocks.

Spectacular.

Lilly placed her hands on her hips. "Quit looking at me like that."

"I can't help it. But seriously, I'm not sure how the people in the boat behind us will feel when we don't move out of the way for them soon. The only thing I can do is blame the stubborn American woman. I hope they'll understand."

Lilly glanced back at the other boat. There were at least ten people staring in her direction. The skipper of the other boat gave a gesture with his hand to tell them to get moving. Then he honked the horn on the boat.

Marco turned back at the other boat and yelled. "We can't go until she kisses me."

Lilly bent down and smacked Marco on the arm. "I can't believe you!"

"Kiss him," several people on the other boat yelled. Laughter and catcalls came next as the skipper honked the horn and they chanted. "Bacci! Bacci! Bacci!"

Marco smirked. "Wow, they really want us to kiss, imagine that? You know you want to, so you might as well just do it. Life is passing you by, Lilly Jones. Live a little."

She looked back at the other boat again, then turned to Marco. "Stand up."

Marco grinned. "It would be a pleasure." He stood and took a step toward Lilly. "Now what?"

"Be quiet—that's what." Lilly stepped closer to Marco and ran her hands up his arms, across his chest, and then continued upward until they wrapped around his neck. "You're bad."

He shrugged. "It's your fault. You and your——"

"Shut up so I can kiss you."

"Of cour——"

Lilly yanked Marco's head, stood on her tiptoes and kissed him.

She felt so good in his arms.

The perfect size. The perfect height. The perfect kiss.

Lilly pulled away from the kiss and smiled.

Cheers echoed underneath the archway from the other boat. Dominic joined in the fun, cheering them on and honking the horn.

Startled by the excruciating noise of the horn, Lilly jumped and lost her balance. She latched onto Marco's arms with her death grip and fell backward, the force pulling them both over the edge of the boat and into the water.

Lilly came up for air and let out a loud gasp. She cleared the hair from her eyes and glared at Marco. "This is all your fault." She slapped water in his face. "Look what you've done."

He floated closer, inches from her face. "Me? You're the one who lost her balance." He slapped water back at her.

"You're the one who insisted on the kiss!" She slapped water at him again. "What do you have to say for yourself?"

He grinned. "What a kiss."

She slapped water in his face again, but then screamed. "Ouch! I think I got bit by something."

He chuckled. "Right. Must be the infamous Italian

piranha." Marco felt a sharp sting on his leg. "Shit! Something got me too."

"Ahhh!" Lilly yelled even louder. "That hurts like a—ahhh!"

Marco screamed as he felt a couple more stings. "What the hell is that?"

Dominic pointed from the boat to the water and screamed. "Get out of the water. Jellyfish. There must be ten of them." He threw a bright orange life ring connected to a rope toward Lilly and smacked her on the side of the head with it.

Marco grabbed Lilly with one arm and the life ring with the other as Dominic pulled them back to the boat. Then Marco grabbed Lilly by the waist and pushed her up toward Dominic's extended arms. The force of trying to get her out pushed him under the water.

Then he felt another sting on the side of his arm.

The pain was excruciating, but he resurfaced and coughed. He took a deep breath and lunged for the edge of the boat, pulling himself up in one swift motion, without Dominic's help.

Lilly was on her back on the floor of the boat.

Dominic squatted and pointed to the purplish tracks on her legs where she was stung. "We need to get her to a hospital."

Chapter Thirteen

"That was so much fun," Lilly said, making sure her words had plenty of sarcasm as they left the hospital. "Hey, I have an idea. Let's go find some beehives to disturb."

Marco didn't answer. Smart man.

"Stung by jellyfish and then three hours in the hospital..." She shook her head and continued walking ahead of Marco back down toward the water. "That's what I get for being spontaneous."

"That kiss was amazing."

Lilly stopped and turned back to Marco. "Is that all you can think about?"

"*You're* all I think about."

She didn't answer, even though it was one of the most romantic things she'd ever heard. She had to focus on the matter at hand. Finding Roberto.

They talked with a few locals by the fish market who knew the Rossi family and where their property was. It shouldn't have been a surprise since the entire island was the size of Central Park in New York. Still, that search was in vain when they showed up to an empty house.

Frustrated and tired of complaining, Lilly pointed to a

restaurant. "I'm hungry. Go find out if they have menus or if it's a restaurant for freaks."

Marco eyed the restaurant and then turned back to Lilly. "If we eat here, that would mean you are being spontaneous again. Sure you want to do that?"

"Now!"

Marco didn't respond but she could have sworn she heard laughter coming from him as he went inside the restaurant. A minute later, he popped his head outside. "Menus."

"Good," Lilly said, now feeling guilty for talking to him that way. She entered the restaurant and pointed to the corner. "I need to use the restroom. I'll be back."

She waited for Marco to make a snide remark but he remained quiet. She entered the bathroom and before she sat on the toilet, she checked to make sure there was toilet paper.

"Two rolls," she said, a little too loudly. She'd better not hear a knock on the door.

A few minutes later she joined Marco at a cute little table for two by the open window.

Marco stood, a worried look on his face. Cute.

He pulled out the chair for Lilly and gestured for her to sit. "You okay?"

"I'm fine," she said, trying to forget about what happened with the jellyfish even though the pain in her legs was a constant reminder. And why wasn't he suffering as much as she was? It wasn't fair.

She picked up the menu and studied the various choices, noticing in her peripheral vision that Marco hadn't picked up his menu. He sat there, quiet, staring at her.

"What's the problem?" asked Lilly.

He stared at her for another moment and scratched the side of his face. "I don't know. I'm just expecting for you to threaten to go back to Rome."

She shook her head. "We need to find Roberto. After dinner, we'll grab the ferry to Positano and look for him." But she didn't want to talk about Roberto at the moment. She pointed out the window. "Those look like rain clouds."

Marco turned to look. "Glad we saw Faraglione before it got rough out there."

"Would you like to die a slow death or shall I make it instant?" She didn't like her tone and felt guilty again. "Sorry. I'm not a fan of jellyfish stings and hospitals, that's all."

"Understood."

She stared out at the dark clouds again. "It really looks like a nasty storm is about to hit."

"You're right. Sometimes they have to shut down the ferries crossing back and forth because of the weather. It's rare, but it happens."

Lilly continued to stare out the window. She didn't think it would happen to them, would it? She wasn't going to worry about that at the moment. She was starving and would kill someone if she didn't get food in her system soon. They would enjoy a nice meal and then make their way to Positano to find Roberto.

Fifteen minutes later, the waiter brought their food and placed it on the table—oven-baked red snapper, baby tomatoes and pan-fried potatoes. Then he pointed to the window. "I need to move your table and close that. A storm is coming."

It was a good idea since Lilly had already felt sprinkles on her arm.

Marco and Lilly stood back as the waiter pulled their table away from the window. He closed the window and gestured for them to sit again. Not a minute later, the window was pounded with rain.

"This is amazing," Lilly said, watching the raindrops hit the window and slide down to the bottom of the glass. "It was sunny thirty minutes ago."

"This is very rare. I think the last time I saw this happen in the summer was about ten years ago."

The waiter returned and filled their water glasses. "You have a good memory. I remember it well since it was the first day I worked here. Coincidentally this is my last day working here, so it must be that the storms come and go when I do!" The waiter laughed but Lilly didn't find that funny at all. "And it looks like this will be the storm of the century. My boss told me they stopped all travel to the mainland."

"Of course they did," Lilly said, shaking her head and wondering what else could go wrong.

They needed to get off Capri and over to Positano to find Roberto. Now what was she going to do?

"I know what you're thinking," said Marco, wiping his mouth.

"No, you don't."

"Sure, I do. You want to get to Positano and you are wondering what we're going to do now."

"You got me in this mess and you're getting me out of it. If the boats are not running, we'll rent a helicopter."

"No way would they fly in these conditions. I mean, look. It's getting worse."

Many of the trees were blowing sideways, and the rain was coming down even harder.

Lilly placed her napkin on the table. "How is this possible? It looks like a tropical storm and we are not even in the tropics. It makes no sense."

Marco reached across the table and placed his hand on top of Lilly's. "Don't worry. As soon as it's safe, we'll be on the first boat to Positano. Promise."

Lilly hoped so, but she had a bad feeling about this. Not lactose-intolerant-bad, but still bad. The worst part of all was she couldn't do a thing about it. It was out of her hands. The only thing she could do now was try to enjoy the meal and relax.

Good luck with that.

Forty-five minutes later, they had finished their wonderful meal and headed out into the rain without an umbrella. They tried to stay as close to the buildings as possible after ducking down one street.

Marco waved Lilly into a salmon-colored building with a large white awning. "Here. Come on."

They entered the lobby and Lilly stopped walking when she saw the reception desk. "A hotel?"

"Yes."

"What are we doing here?"

Marco shrugged. "Well, we have no way to get off the island. What else are we going to do? Sleep on the street in the rain?"

"I told you—we're not spending the night in Capri. We need to get out of here."

"And I told *you* that's impossible. We're stuck on one of the most beautiful islands in the world, so you'll just have to deal with it. Enjoy it, even. Fortunately, I know someone who works here."

"You know someone who works everywhere."

"Very funny. I'll get us two rooms, so stay put and I'll be right back."

Lilly plopped down in a comfy gold chair by the oval window and sighed. Raindrops danced on the tile outside. The sound was soothing, and she felt sleepy.

Marco was sure he knew what Lilly's reaction would be like

when he gave her the news. She would not be happy. He turned away from the reception desk of the hotel and approached her.

She sat with her eyes closed in the waiting area. She looked breathtaking. He stood in front of her, not wanting to disturb her. This was a great way to delay the news.

She opened her eyes and glared at him. "How long have you been standing there?"

"About an hour."

She laughed and stood, wiping her eyes. "Right." She grabbed the handle of her carryon. "Ready?"

Here we go. Good luck.

"Kind of…" Marco said, once again trying to delay the inevitable.

"I don't like that look on your face. What happened? Don't tell me they don't have rooms."

"They have rooms. Well…" He grimaced. "One room."

"What do you mean one room?"

Marco held up a single key card and forced a grin. "One."

"No, no, no, no," Lilly said, waving her finger at Marco. "Nice try. We are not sleeping in the same bed."

"Lilly Pilly, what kind of man do you take me for?"

"A man is a man. Just like a goat is a goat."

Marco laughed. "I don't understand what that means, but there are two beds in the room and we have no other options. All the other hotels are sold out, and we got the last room here. They had to put all of those people from boats somewhere. So quit complaining and follow me."

"I like to complain. I'm good at complaining."

"No argument there."

"Hey—watch it." She glanced over at the reception desk. "I'll be back. There has to be another room and I will get it."

Marco sat in the chair. "Good luck. You'll need it."

Lilly approached the man at the reception desk and spoke with him. Marco couldn't hear the conversation but the man shook his head now. A few more words and then another shake of the head and a frown from the man. Lilly turned around and walked back to Marco.

Marco stood and couldn't help what was about to come out of his mouth. "Did you get the presidential suite?"

"Stuff a sock in it and take me to our room."

As difficult as it was, Marco kept the laughter inside and stood, leading Lilly toward the elevator.

They went up to the fourth floor and headed down the hallway to their room. Marco slid the key into the slot on the door and quickly pulled it out. The green light lit on the lock and he cranked the door open and pushed it forward. "After you..."

Lilly squeezed by Marco and rolled her suitcase against the wall. She turned toward the window and sighed. "Oh wow."

Marco pulled his suitcase into the room and let the door slide closed behind him. He moved to Lilly's side and stared out the window at their view. "I agree. Wow."

Even on a rainy day the Mediterranean was a sight to see. The trees swayed back and forth in the wind and the raindrops hitting the window sounded like someone lightly tapping their fingernails against the glass.

Lilly turned toward the two double beds. "Oh…"

"What? Not what you expected?"

Lilly continued to stare at the bed. "Okay, this wasn't planned well and I don't have anything appropriate to sleep in."

"You forgot to bring pajamas or…what do you women call those things? Nightshirts?"

"Well…I…"

She was hiding something. "What?" Then it came to him. "Oh. You sleep in the nude?" Just the thought of Lilly naked in his bed got his pulse going.

"Dream on. My nightgown was meant to be seen only by me."

"How do you know it was only meant to be seen by you?"

"I'm a woman. I know."

"Well, I'm a man and I'll be the judge of that. Show me."

Lilly grabbed the pillow from the bed and threw it at Marco. "So typical."

"No. Typical would be a man who stares. I would just sneak a peek and give you my honest opinion, that's all."

"And you don't think I'd notice you sneaking a peek?"

He shook his head. "I'm really sneaky."

Lilly laughed. "Okay, well it doesn't matter because it's not going to happen, so get that out of your mind."

"It's completely erased," he lied. "Wait…" He opened his suitcase and moved things aside, pulling out a t-shirt. He threw it to her. "You can wear this if it makes you feel more comfortable."

She unfolded the t-shirt and read the front. "Just Do It." She smirked. "I should have known."

Marco laughed. "You have a dirty mind, you know that? I bought that t-shirt because it's positive, it encourages, and it's motivating."

Lilly stared at him for a moment, looking like she almost believed him. "If you say so. Look, I don't know if it's from the full stomach or the Benadryl…maybe it's from the jetlag or almost being killed by jellyfish, but I'm tired and just would like to crawl into bed and sleep. Is that okay?"

"Of course."

Lilly grabbed a few things from her suitcase and went into the bathroom. Marco used the time to change out of his clothes before she came back out, although he was presented with a problem.

Unlike Lilly, he slept in the buff.

Chapter Fourteen

Lilly woke up and peeked over at Marco, who was still asleep. The bedcover wasn't completely over him and she could see one side of his chest, abs, and the top part of his hip. Was he sleeping in the nude? It sure seemed like it. She shook her head, wanting so much to lift that cover. Or maybe she should just set off the fire alarm so he jumped out of bed. Just the thought made her giggle. She threw her hand over mouth.

She shook the thoughts of a naked Marco out of her head. Now was her chance to get to the bathroom and change out of his t-shirt before she got another one of those looks from him.

God, the way he looked at Lilly melted her.

Last night, she wanted to slip out of that t-shirt and into his bed. To say she was attracted to Marco would be an understatement. To say she didn't dream about him last night would be a lie. But it was best to forget about that dream and get to the business at hand. Tracking down Roberto and saving the company.

Lilly changed out of the t-shirt and washed her face.

"You okay, Lilly?" said Marco from the other side of the

door, not having the decency to stay asleep until she had finished.

"I'm fine," Lilly said, wondering if he was out there in his underwear or naked. "Be right out."

She was tempted to open the door for a little look-see, but that wouldn't be smart.

"Take your time," Marco said. "Just wanted to make sure, considering what happened in Rome."

She didn't even want to think about that. "Got it. I'm hoping that was a once-in-a-lifetime event."

Marco didn't answer.

A few seconds later, she opened the bathroom door and froze. "Oh…"

Marco was pulling up his jeans over his red boxer briefs and looked up. "Sorry. I thought you'd be in there a little longer. Let me just…" He pulled up the jeans and zipped them closed.

Lilly pulled her suitcase from the closet floor and closed the door, careful to keep her attention away from the hot Italian man who was still shirtless.

She had forgotten about the mirrors on the closet doors and was just given a beautiful view of Marco stretching his arms over his head to slide on his t-shirt.

Too bad he caught her looking.

"Sorry," said Marco again, pulling the t-shirt down over his waist. "All done."

A pity.

Lilly handed him back his t-shirt she had worn to bed. "Thank you."

She should have smelled it one more time but that would've been wrong.

Marco placed the t-shirt in his carry-on. "You're welcome."

"Quick breakfast and off to Positano?" she asked. They had to get moving.

"Yes. Breakfast comes with the room, so we can head down now and be on our way within an hour." He pointed out the window to the Mediterranean Sea. "Beautiful day. Zero chance of not making it across."

"Good."

Marco grinned and took a few steps toward Lilly. "And don't worry—I didn't forget about the grapes."

Lilly was confused. "Grapes?"

"You know… Last night you asked me if I would hand-feed grapes to you while you reclined on the terrace. It would be a pleasure."

She stared at him for a moment, wondering if he was joking or if she had talked in her sleep again. A few seconds later she got her answer when he laughed. Lilly grabbed a pillow from the bed and flung it as hard as she could, connecting with his face.

A little over an hour later they were on a boat crossing back over to the mainland. They had eaten quickly, some toast and eggs, and even went online for a few minutes to search for Roberto's family's property.

Marco eyed the mainland as they cruised closer on the ferry. "Are we all set with the plan?"

Lilly nodded. "I think so. We're lucky that Positano is small." There were only fifteen Rossi families in Positano, according to the man at the front desk. How he knew that Lilly hadn't a clue, but the guy said that everyone knew everyone on Positano. Just like in Capri.

Lilly glanced over at Marco, who was staring at her. "What?"

He shrugged. "Have I told you how beautiful you are?"

"Yes. This morning. Yesterday. And I think the day before too. Quit flirting with me."

"Flirting? I'm not flirting. I'm just stating a fact. Facts are readily available and I'm not the only one who thinks you're beautiful." Marco tapped the man to his side on the shoulder.

"Marco, what are you doing?"

"Proving a point."

"Stop it."

The man turned around.

Marco pointed to Lilly. "Do you think this woman is beautiful?"

The man eyed Lilly and nodded. "Bella!"

Marco smirked. "Thank you." He turned back to Lilly. "See?"

"Is she single?" asked the man.

"As a matter of fact…"

"No," Lilly screamed. "I'm not single." She grabbed Marco by the arm and yanked him closer. "Please don't listen to him."

The man scooted away, obviously annoyed with the game Lilly and Marco were playing. Lilly didn't like it very much either.

She let go of his arm and then smacked him on it. "Knock it off."

"What? I did nothing wrong. You are a beautiful, single, albeit kind of crazy woman…"

She smacked him again. "Hey."

"I was just trying to help you find that husband you're looking for. And why do you want a husband so badly, anyway?"

"God, you make me sound desperate."

"You're definitely on a mission, so there must be a reason, right?"

"Why can't a woman want to have love in her life, a husband, a family?"

"That sounds wonderful. But what I'm trying to ask is… why the urgency? Is this one of those my-clock-is-ticking-so-I-better-get-going things? Because you're young. You have all the time in the world."

Right. That she didn't have.

She wanted to do couples things with other couples. Barbecues. Birthday parties for the kids. She wanted to be a soccer mom and talk on the sidelines with the other soccer moms about funny TV shows and their annoying husbands.

She was dying to have an annoying husband.

All of Lilly's best friends were married, most of them with children now. She wanted that. She was ready. She didn't want to have toddlers when all of her friends had teenagers. But maybe it wasn't the best time to think about that since a certain Italian man was staring at her.

She tucked some hair behind her ear and Marco laughed. "Be quiet."

He reached over and tucked the hair on the other side of her face behind her ear. "You missed some." He continued to laugh.

Lilly felt her face getting hotter. "Knock it off. And what about you? You're a handsome guy..."

He cocked his head to the side and grinned. "Are you saying you're attracted to me, Lilly?"

Men. "Answer the question."

"I don't think there was a question."

"Let me be direct. Why aren't you married with a zoo of children?"

Marco shrugged. "My lifestyle doesn't warrant it."

"Then why don't you change your lifestyle?"

He thought about it for a few seconds. "Good question. And the answer is...I don't know. I guess I still haven't gotten my career in place yet, so I'm not so sure I should put focus on another area until I figure that out."

"You can't chew gum and ride your bike at the same time?"

"I don't have a bike."

"You know what I mean."

He looked out at the water and sighed. "Honestly, I don't think there has ever been anyone who had ever motivated me enough to want to consider a serious relationship and change my focus."

Marco didn't like that disappointed look on Lilly's face. The truth was Lilly was the only one who ever made him think of having a serious relationship, but there was no way he would tell her that. It was almost time for him to go to Australia and she needed to find Roberto Rossi and get back to work. And who knew if she thought Roberto was her future husband.

It was obvious to Marco that he and Lilly had serious chemistry, more than he'd had with any woman, but was that enough? Did people just put everything else on hold or push it to the side and choose love? What about his career? Yes, it was true—he could work just about anywhere. And he had enough experience to work in several fields, but what about his goals? His dreams? At the moment, they didn't seem that big at all because all he could think about was Lilly.

Lilly was gorgeous. Smart. Crazy.

He'd never get bored with her, that's for sure. But he

needed to stop driving himself nuts with his thoughts. This wasn't going to happen. She was focused on finding Roberto and that was that.

They disembarked from the ferry and Marco pointed to the Vespa Rental sign. "There. Let's go."

Lilly stopped. "Tell me you're kidding."

"Why would I kid about something like that? It's the easiest way to get around. Cheap. No trouble finding parking. Plus, it's fun!" He grinned. "Sounds like a win to me."

"You failed to mention the part about us dying on that thing."

Marco chuckled. "I doubt we'll get in a serious accident at the terrifying high speed of fifteen miles per hour. Some people can walk that fast."

"Then let's walk."

"Do you want to find your future lover or not?"

"I'm not beyond punching you."

"I know, but let's go. Time's wasting away and you're on a mission."

Lilly didn't respond and followed Marco to the Vespa counter to rent the scooter. The truth was he couldn't wait to rent it. Scooters were so much fun and the thought of having Lilly's arms and legs wrapped around him had him as giddy as a kid at Disneyland. But he wasn't going to let her know that.

They left their suitcases in the lockers at the rental shop, grabbed their helmets and headed back outside to get on the scooter.

Marco pointed to the Vespa and smiled. "Red. My favorite color."

She already knew based on her reaction that morning when she saw him pulling his jeans over his red boxer shorts in the hotel room. He didn't mean for her to see or for her to be uncomfortable but he loved that she stole a few glances. Even a couple of looks in the mirror. Maybe she didn't think he could see it, but he saw it all right.

Lilly slid the open face helmet on and Marco reached over without thinking and secured the chin strap for her. He was almost certain she was acting a little shy.

"Thank you," she said. "Great service here."

"Please let me know if you need anything else."

Like a back rub. A few kisses. A massage.

Okay, he needed to just stop torturing himself.

He slid his helmet on, secured the chin strap, and sat down on the scooter, keeping both legs planted to the ground for balance. "Hop on."

Lilly didn't hesitate, swinging her leg over the back of the seat. She scooted closer and wrapped her arms around his midsection. Then she inched closer so her chest was plastered to his back.

I could get used to this. Maybe I'll just take my time.

"Why aren't we going anywhere yet?" she asked. "We need to get moving."

Okay. Maybe he wouldn't take his time. Better get a

move on.

"Right," he said, starting the engine and easing onto the crowded street with the other scooters and cars. It was only a two-lane road, so it wasn't difficult. The thing to watch out for were the other people on scooters, typically the younger kids, who liked to weave in and out of traffic.

"This is beautiful," Lilly said as they wound through the hills up above Positano.

Marco pulled over for a second to admire the view. "Take a picture."

"Great idea!"

A minute later they were back on the road and pulling up to the Rossi property. Was this *the* Rossi property, the one with the man she was looking for? Only time would tell, but it didn't appear so, since there were no cars there and the blinds were shut. The house had all the classic personality traits of the other homes in Positano. Beautiful, colorful, a salmon color with red trim. And lots of flowers and native plants.

Marco maneuvered the Vespa closer to the front of the house and pointed to the large dark brown front door. "It doesn't look like anyone is here, but go knock on the front door just in case."

Lilly slid off the back, keeping her helmet on, and knocked on the front door. Then she knocked again. A few seconds later she shrugged and returned to the scooter. She didn't say a word and avoided eye contact with him. She slid back on and wrapped her hands around his waist for the second time. And for the second time he enjoyed it, maybe even more this round.

He cranked his head so she could hear okay. "Don't worry, we'll find him. The other place is just around the corner."

Two minutes later, they pulled up to the next property. It looked almost identical to the first house. But the color of the house was more of an orange and it had the same classic roof with the Spanish style tile.

A cute Italian boy, maybe eight or nine years old, came from the house. His eyes were wide, filled with curiosity.

Marco asked the boy if this was the Rossi home and the boy smiled, answered yes, and pointed to the house.

Marco didn't like the feeling in his gut. There was someone home there. Two Fiats were in the driveway next to a BMW. He wanted Lilly to find her man. On the other hand, he didn't want her to find him. That would mean an end to their trip. An end to their time together. And an end to their relationship.

Chapter Fifteen

Lilly slid off the Vespa and removed her helmet. Marco had confirmed with the boy that Roberto Rossi's grandparents lived in the house. *The* Roberto Rossi she was looking for.

She should be excited. She should be relieved. But she was neither.

Lilly was used to having Marco around.

But she had a company to save. And what about finding her husband? Was Roberto the one? Could it be possible that Madam Love was right with her crazy predictions? The bear, the expensive car, and the trip out of the country to find the love of her life? And she still didn't understand how a temple played a part of it all.

The boy ran inside the home and returned a few seconds later with an older man, most likely Roberto's grandfather.

"I am Roberto," he said, a proud smile on his face. "Nicoli tells me you are looking for my grandson, Roberto."

Lilly nodded. "Yes. We were supposed to meet in Rome but I couldn't make it. Is he here?"

Roberto frowned. "I'm sorry, but he is not. He left for Sorrento this morning and will spend two nights there. There is some type of, how do you say? Corporate event, I think.

Samsung. They make the beautiful televisions."

Lilly knew who Samsung was and how beautiful their televisions were. That didn't matter at this point. But now she had to wonder if he already accepted the offer from Samsung. It sure sounded like he had, but she couldn't take a chance. She needed to do everything possible to get him back to the US.

"Where is the event?" Lilly said, hoping his grandfather wouldn't mind sharing. It's not like Lilly and Marco looked like psychos or anything.

"The Hotel...hmm, which hotel is that? Just one moment." He walked to the front door, swung it open, and yelled something in Italian."

"He's asking the family if they know the hotel," Marco said.

Lilly nodded, hoping they knew something. Otherwise, what was she going to do now? She knew one thing was for sure, Marco would be the one taking her to Sorrento. He wasn't off the hook yet, which was a good thing. More time with Marco felt like a good thing, but she was just delaying the inevitable.

Roberto closed the front door behind him and smiled. "Hotel Florence in Sorrento. Downtown. You can't miss it. It's the one with a beautiful fountain."

Lilly wasn't going to tell him that just about every hotel in Italy had a fountain.

"I know it," said Marco.

"He is at an event, so you have a few hours before you can see him."

"That's perfect. We can stop and see Stefano and Daniella. We can call him on the way. Grazie." They said goodbye to Roberto and Marco grabbed his helmet. "Okay, Sorrento, here we come."

They headed back down the hill on the Vespa and returned the scooter to the rental office. Lilly knew they wouldn't be using it to go to Sorrento. The easiest way was to take the bus and there were buses leaving all the time.

They grabbed their suitcases from the man at the rental office and made their way to the bus station. Twenty minutes later, they boarded the bus to Sorrento.

It was sinking in now. They were certain Roberto was at the Hotel Florence and that was most likely where Marco and Lilly would say goodbye.

This was just weird and sad.

The closer they got to Sorrento, the more knots she had in her stomach. She didn't want to say goodbye to Marco, but she knew it was the right thing to do. He couldn't be her future husband. He was going to Australia and who knew if he would ever return? She went through the heartbreak of two people disappearing from her life and she wouldn't allow herself to go through it again.

The bus station was just around the corner, so it took two minutes on foot to get to Stefano's house. The front door swung open before Marco could knock on it.

An Italian man smiled, holding his arms out. "Glad you could make it, my friend."

Marco smiled, hugging Stefano and kissing him on both cheeks. "You too. It's been too long. Lilly, this is my best friend, Stefano."

Stefano stepped toward Lilly and kissed her on both cheeks. "Bella. Such a pleasure to meet you. Marco has told me so much about you."

Surprised, Lilly swung around to Marco. "When was this?"

Marco shrugged, but didn't answer.

"Today. Yesterday." continued Stefano, with a surprising amount of enthusiasm. "Text messages. Some with smiley faces and hearts and—"

"Okay, okay," said Marco, throwing up his hands and calling for a timeout. "Stefano is exaggerating. We may have exchanged a few words. I don't even recall."

Stefano slapped Marco on the back. "There is nothing to be ashamed about, my friend. Love is a beautiful thing. Please come inside."

Love is a beautiful thing?

Why did Stefano say that? Marco didn't love her. Yes, she could tell he was into her, but love? Absurd.

The house was gorgeous, just like the Italian homes Lilly had seen on television and in the movies. Lots of colors, yellow, green, red. And tiles. Tiles everywhere.

They stepped out onto the back patio and a woman with

olive skin and dark hair turned, smiling at Marco. Her gaze shifted over to Lilly, checking her out from head to toe. She must have wondered who this American girl was and why she was with Marco.

"This must be Lilly," she said, an even bigger smile on her face. "I'm Daniella, Marco's sister."

"Oh…" Lilly said, being pulled in tight for an embrace, followed by two kisses on the cheeks. "Hello…"

Daniella gently pushed Lilly away and glanced down at her feet, then moved upward all the way to her hair. "Just as Marco said…bella!"

Lilly turned to Marco. How many people had he talked to about her and how come she never noticed? And why was he talking about her so much?

Marco shrugged. "Did I say she was beautiful? Hmm. Don't remember."

"Ha!" said Daniella, pinching her brother in his side. "He also told me about the restaurant—you poor thing— and the jellyfish and the kiss. Don't worry, we won't have any dairy products in the pasta for dinner."

Marco turned to Stefano. "Doesn't anyone value private conversations anymore?"

Daniella laughed and linked arms with Lilly. "My brother is a good man. A little closed off sometimes, but a good man."

Lilly had to agree he was a very good man and was flattered he'd been talking about her.

Stefano poured glasses of wine for everyone and they toasted to happiness.

Daniella squeezed Lilly's arm. "How long will you be in Italy, Lilly?"

Lilly crinkled her nose. "I leave tomorrow."

"You don't look too happy about that. You've been enjoying your time with my brother, I take it?"

Lilly nodded and glanced over at Marco. "Very much. But, as the saying goes, all good things must end."

"I don't like that saying at all," Marco said, looking eager to give his opinion. He held out his wine glass to Lilly, Daniella, and Stefano who approached again. "Life is not measured by the amount of breaths you take, but by the moments that take your breath away."

They all clinked glasses and Daniella lit up. "Marco! This is beautiful."

Lilly rolled her eyes. "Don't be too impressed. That was a quote from the movie *Hitch*. We watched it on the flight here from San Francisco."

Marco waved his finger at Lilly. "You shouldn't give away all my secrets."

Daniella laughed. "I love this woman, Marco."

"Me too," said Marco, losing his smile when Daniella lit up. "I mean…she's great."

Marco took a sip of his wine and looked away.

Damn. Why did I say that?

Marco continued to look away, hoping Lilly didn't notice.

The truth was he had feelings for Lilly. Strong feelings. When he said he loved her too he meant... Oh hell, who knew what he meant? Maybe it was the kind of love people associate with their favorite things.

I love pasta.

I love to travel.

I love Lilly.

He shook his head. The last one felt different when it went through his mind.

Crap.

Now he wanted to kiss her. *Needed* to kiss her. That was the only thing running through his mind.

"Would you like more wine?" Marco asked, trying to get her lips off his mind.

Lilly stared at her full glass of wine and laughed. "You're obviously trying to get me drunk or maybe you're pushing the wine again. Is this from your winery?"

"No," he said, not sure what else to say. What would she think if he grabbed her right there and kissed her? Should he ask her first? She objected to his kisses more than a few times in the last couple of days. "Can I speak to you for a moment?"

Lilly looked around and then made eye contact with Marco. "Was that a trick question? You *are* speaking with me."

Marco let out a nervous chuckle. Why was he so nervous? Maybe he knew if he kissed her again it would feel different this time. Because his feelings had changed. They were stronger.

He was falling in love with her.

Hell, forget about falling. He already fell.

Hard.

Maybe he was the one who needed more wine.

He slammed the rest of his glass and set it on the table. "Come with me, please." He grabbed Lilly's hand and pulled her toward the fig tree in the corner of the yard.

Lilly smiled and pointed to the tree. "You going to pick fruit?"

He shook his head. "There's something else I want that's a lot sweeter."

He leaned forward and kissed Lilly, pulling her closer. He deepened the kiss when she responded positively by running her fingers across the back of his neck and through the hair above the back of his shirt collar. A good sign.

She was enjoying it as much as he was.

He had to tell her he loved her. He didn't know how she'd react but he had to. Now was the perfect time.

Or maybe not.

Stefano came back out from the house and rang the cowbell, startling both Marco and Lilly. "Okay, my friends. We have pasta, pasta, and pasta. Buon appetito!"

<<<>>>

Lilly broke off the wonderful kiss with Marco with the sound of the cowbell and they turned back toward the house. Stefano and Daniella waved them over for dinner even though she would have been happy continuing that kiss.

That kiss.

She wanted more, but the moment was gone.

Stefano gestured toward the table with the plates and food. "Please help yourself."

Marco grabbed two plates. "I'm starving." He handed a plate to Lilly. "I hope you're hungry."

"Thank you. I'm starving."

They filled their plates with food and sat.

Lilly scooted her chair in and brushed arms with Marco.

"What?" Marco said.

"I didn't say anything."

"You looked like you wanted to."

"Nope."

Marco nodded and took a bite of his salad.

"That must be so wonderful that your best friend is married to your sister," Lilly said.

Marco smiled and winked at his sister. "It's the best."

"Was he your best friend before they dated?"

"No. He was a wine distributor who I did business with. One of the nicest, most honest guys and—"

"You introduced them?"

Daniella nodded. "He made sure we were in the same place at the same time. Marco was having a special wine event and invited us both. He's sneaky but I will never complain."

Stefano passed the bread to Daniella and then dropped his hand below the table to Daniella's lap.

Sweet. They looked happy. In love.

She wanted that.

She glanced over to Marco.

"You're doing it again," Marco said, this time grinning. "Are you going to say what's on your mind or pretend it was nothing?"

"I'll pretend. But I was just thinking…you're a matchmaker. Like Hitch."

Marco chuckled. "Not quite." He shrugged. "Okay. Maybe I am…"

"You are. And you're a romantic too—quoting Will Smith like that." Lilly laughed and took a bite of her pasta.

"Okay, now you're making fun of me."

"Nooooo. Me?"

They laughed and enjoyed dinner with Stefano and Daniella.

Later after the plates were cleared, they sipped on dessert wine, continuing to chat about life and love.

"What do you do in the States, Lilly?" Stefano asked.

"I work at a high tech company in Silicon Valley. I'm

Vice President of Human Resources."

Stefano nodded, a confused look on his face. "I find it odd they need to clarify that the resources are for humans. Do you have animals working for your company?"

Lilly laughed. "Sometimes it seems like it." Her phone sounded from an incoming text. "I'm so sorry. I think this is work related."

"It's okay," Daniella said.

Lilly pulled the phone from her purse. The text was from Roberto.

My grandfather said you stopped by. I'm staying at Hotel Florence in Sorrento, if you'd like to call or stop by. Room 227. It would be great to see you.

Lilly read the text again. Roberto seemed eager to see her, which was a great sign.

"Everything okay?" asked Marco.

Lilly nodded. "It's from Roberto. He's at the hotel and said I can stop by now." She glanced over at Daniella and Stefano. "This has been a wonderful evening. Unfortunately, I must go."

Daniella frowned. "You can't stay a little longer? We have an extra bedroom, so you can stay the night with us. I'd love that."

"I'd love it too, but if I don't get this contract signed I won't have a job because we won't have a company. How long does it take to get to Hotel Florence from here?"

"About thirty minutes," said Daniella. "Twenty minutes if my brother is driving."

Marco shook his head. "Very funny, but we took the bus."

Stefano pushed his plate to the center of the table and stood. "Not a problem. Take my car." He pulled the keys from his pocket and tossed them to Marco. "It was a pleasure having you here, Lilly, and you're welcome back anytime. With or without Marco."

"Hey!" said Marco, pretending to be hurt by that comment.

Lilly would love to return with Marco. But that wasn't realistic. Was the ride to the hotel going to be the last time they saw each other? The last few days with Marco had been the best and all she wanted now was for him to say something, anything that would give her hope. Hope that there was a way they could see each other. A way for them to be together.

That look on his face wasn't a good sign.

Chapter Sixteen

Marco said little as he drove Lilly to the hotel. Neither did she. If he wanted to say something, he'd better hurry. They had about ten minutes until they got there. But what would he say?

Say something. Anything.

Marco pointed out the window. "Even beautiful at night, isn't it?"

That's what you wanted to say? You've spent the most amazing few days with the woman of your dreams and you want to talk about things out the window? Wake up and smell the cappuccino!

Lilly was deep in thought, turning to Marco. "Yeah..." Her energy was low, almost nonexistent. "Gorgeous." She turned and stared out the window again.

"Like you..."

Better. A little cliché but not bad.

"Thank you. And thank you for your help. I know I messed up your vacation."

Did she really think that? Wasn't she even aware of how much he enjoyed her company? How much he didn't want to say goodbye? How much he enjoyed kissing her?

Tell her.

"You didn't mess up my vacation. I thought it was obvious how much fun I had with you."

She shrugged but didn't reply.

"So…what's the plan?" he asked, hoping to at least get the conversation a little deeper before they arrived.

"Well…talk with Roberto. Get him to accept the job offer and then…go back home."

"You don't have time to see anything else?"

"My flight isn't until six in the evening, so I think I'll see the Trevi Fountain in the afternoon right before I go."

"Are you going to re-enact a scene from a movie? Maybe take a dip in the water?"

She chuckled. "Not quite. I don't want to get arrested on my last day. But it would be nice to see it."

Marco's heart rate picked up as he pulled into the parking lot of the hotel. He should ask to see her again back in the States. Get together for a beer or a glass of wine or kissing. Lots of kissing. Or maybe they could spend a few hundred months together. But he had to go to Australia. He didn't want to go—had no interest. What was he going to say?

Tell her you love her.

Like that would go over well.

Hey, Lilly. I love you. I'll see you in six months!

Right. Like she would go for that. She could get any guy she wanted. And even though Marco knew they had serious chemistry why would she wait for him?

They entered the lobby of the hotel and Lilly pointed to the phone on the wall. "Roberto gave me his room number. I can just call from there." She stared at Marco, looking like she wanted to say something else. "Well…" She shrugged and her gaze dropped to his mouth.

And Marco knew if he kissed her, he wouldn't want to leave. But that's just it…he had to leave.

This is torture. At least tell her how you feel. You love her. You know you do. Tell her.

Lilly waited for Marco to say something that would make her believe that they had something special. That they had a future together. She didn't want it to end now, but it sure seemed like it was headed in that direction.

Marco had to go away for work in Australia. It was complicated. She understood that.

He'd hinted at quitting his job but she wouldn't expect him to do that for her. If only she was the kind of woman a man changed his mind about, changing everything because of her. If only she knew his feelings.

Lilly's feelings were clear.

She loved him.

"Lilly…"

Here we go. Tell me something good.

She stepped forward, her eyes feeling a little glossy.

"Yes…"

"I enjoyed your company this week."

"I enjoyed your company too."

He inched forward a little more. "Lilly, I…"

Say it. Tell me what I want to hear. That you want to be with me.

Marco hesitated and then continued. "I want to tell you I —"

"Lilly!" said the male voice from behind Marco. "So glad you could make it!" Roberto approached and kissed Lilly on both cheeks. "You look amazing."

Lilly gave Roberto a half-smile and shot a quick glance over to Marco before returning her attention to Roberto. "You too." She gazed over at Marco again, which caught Roberto's attention.

Roberto pivoted and eyed Marco. "So sorry." He pulled a bill from his wallet and handed it to Marco. "Grazie."

"Oh, no, no," said Lilly. "This is Marco, a…friend. He was kind enough to help me track you down. Marco, this is Roberto."

Roberto pulled the bill back and stuck it in his wallet. Then he extended his hand. "Nice to meet you. And thank you."

"You're welcome."

Marco just stood there staring at Lilly. It didn't appear he would say anything else. That's when she decided she had to protect herself.

If her past was any sign, Marco would do the same thing

Lilly's father did to her. The same thing her last boyfriend did. He would say he was going away for a little while. To Australia.

Then he'd never return.

She couldn't allow herself to go through that again. The pain from someone abandoning her was the worst feeling in the world. Time to cut it off.

"Thank you, Marco," said Lilly, jumping in before the situation got any more awkward. But it got more awkward. Lilly held out her hand.

Marco glanced down at her hand, a confused look on his face. He was obviously not happy with what she was doing. Her way of saying goodbye.

He accepted her handshake. "My pleasure…Lilly." He held onto her hand for a few seconds, squeezing it. Then he kissed it before letting it go.

Lilly fought to hold back the tears.

This was it.

She and Marco didn't have a future together.

Roberto clapped his hands together and gave Lilly a big grin. "Great. How about we grab a drink in the bar and chat then?"

Lilly's gaze traveled to Marco before darting back to Roberto. "Okay…"

"Fantastic. You take care, Marco."

Lilly had lost the energy to do or say anything else. It didn't matter, did it? Roberto grabbed Lilly's bag and rolled it for her toward the bar, Lilly following alongside him.

A few seconds later, she looked back.

Marco was gone.

Forever.

Lilly felt horrible. Why didn't she say anything?

She could have pulled Marco aside and given him a private thank you and a hug. Even a kiss on the cheek. He deserved at least that much.

A handshake? She had no idea what had come over her but it must have been the pressure of Roberto standing there, waiting.

"You seem a little quiet," Roberto said, gesturing to the back of the bar. "You okay?"

"Yeah," she lied, trying to force a smile on her face while picturing Marco.

That look he had on his face as they said goodbye crushed her soul. No. It was like someone took her soul and stuck it in a blender. High speed. No, worse. Puree.

But Marco was gone, and she had to let it go.

Get down to business. Make Roberto the offer. Don't mess around. And get Marco off your mind!

They found a quiet spot in the corner of the bar and Roberto pulled out the chair for Lilly. "Here you go."

"Thank you," she answered, taking a deep breath to calm down. Her blood pressure should be shooting through the roof right about now. "Let's order drinks and then chat about what it will take to get you back to the United States."

"I don't think—"

Lilly held her hand up. "No, no. Drinks first."

Roberto chuckled. "Okay. Drinks first."

The waitress came around, took their orders and a few minutes later the drinks arrived. A vodka tonic for him, a glass of pinot for her. Nothing wrong with helping the wine industry. It was the least she could do considering how she treated Marco.

Roberto held up his drink. "To Italy."

Lilly smiled. "To the United States."

They clinked glasses and laughed, but her thoughts drifted to Marco.

Knock it off. Focus.

"Just one minute." Lilly pulled the paperwork from her bag and handed it to Roberto. "Here you go. Let me know what you think."

Roberto looked at each page, carefully reading them, then going back to the first page and nodding. "How did you manage this? This is thirty percent more than my current offer. How did you know?"

Lilly smiled. "It's my job to know. We want you back— we need you back. The company took a hit after you left and never recovered. We're confident you can get us back on course."

"I'm flattered."

"Good. Let's make this deal then. You'll make many people happy. And then we can celebrate and enjoy the rest of the evening."

He shuffled through the papers again and handed them back to Lilly. "It's not that simple. It's a great offer, but I can't accept it."

Lilly just stared at him. She was certain the wrong words came out of his mouth. He didn't just say he couldn't accept the offer. This was supposed to be a slam dunk.

She took a deep breath, trying to regain her composure. "It's a little noisy in here. It almost sounded like you said you can't accept the offer."

"I can't. I'm sorry. I should have told you Lilly, but we didn't get that much time to talk on the phone when you arrived. There's a girl…"

Oh God, not a girl. Please no. Wrong answer! I don't want to talk about love now!

Lilly sat up in her chair. "It's not serious, is it?"

"I'm going to ask her to marry me. This weekend, in fact."

No, no, no, no. This can't be happening.

"Bring her with you," Lilly said, figuring many people want to come to the United States. "To the US…"

Roberto laughed. "That's not so easy. She has her career here."

"What does she do?"

"She's an engineer."

"Hello? Silicon Valley? Engineer? We can find her a job with a big salary. Huge salary. *Easily.*"

Roberto shook his head. "I'm sorry, Lilly. I can't see this happening. She loves her job here and I don't even think the money would get her to leave. And look at you, coming all this way."

Yeah. Look at me. A fool.

Lilly forced a smile, not sure what else to say. "What's her name?"

"Gabriella."

"Beautiful name. I wish you the best but please let me know if you change your mind. The offer is on the table until Monday, close of business."

Monday.

The day she would be back at work.

Without Roberto.

Without Marco.

Without a clue of what her future held.

She knew one thing though. This was Colette's fault that all of this happened, getting Lilly's hopes up with those ridiculous predictions from Madam Love. The first thing she'd do when she got back was tell Colette off. Or even better, give Madam Love—the fraud—a piece of her mind. Then she would crawl back into her safe little bubble where nobody could hurt her.

Chapter Seventeen

The next day, Lilly didn't feel any better. She'd stayed at Hotel Florence, then she took the first train in the morning back to Rome to her original hotel across from the Colosseum.

All night her thoughts were one hundred percent on Marco.

Wonderful Marco.

Lilly felt like crap the way she said goodbye to him. Marco helped her find Roberto, and she had fun with him. He didn't deserve to be treated that way. He even got Lilly out of her comfort zone and she enjoyed spontaneity for the first time in three years.

The worst thing was she loved Marco. She knew that now, for sure.

I love him.

And he's gone.

She had left her phone on all night hoping that he might call. But why would he? If she were in his position, she wouldn't call.

She blew it.

Lilly left her suitcases with the bellhop. She had a few

hours for lunch and a visit to the Trevi Fountain before she would leave for the airport.

She wandered down a quaint cobblestone street, admiring the cafes and shops along the way. A cute restaurant caught her eye, and she snuck a peek through the window. It looked wonderful, inviting. It was still before noon but she didn't have a problem with an early lunch.

She stepped inside and inhaled.

Wonderful.

Not a surprise there were many smiling faces in the place.

Lilly got the attention of an older gentleman coming from the kitchen with a wave of the hand.

He smiled and approached. "Buon giorno!"

"Buon giorno. Can I look at the menu to see what you have?"

The man shook his head. "I'm sorry but we do not have menus here. You tell us what food you love and the chef will make something special just for you." He gestured to the small table by the window. "Please have a seat. You will love it, I promise you this." He smiled, waiting for Lilly to respond.

Unbelievable. Another restaurant without a menu. Lilly thought of Marco and shook her head. He would tell her to live a little. Quit being so uptight. And she *should* quit being so uptight. What happened in that other restaurant was her own fault for not speaking up. That's all she had to do.

"Do you know what lactose intolerance is?" Lilly asked.

That was smooth. There could have been a better, much smoother way to ask.

"We have a chef who is the best in all of Rome and he will prepare for you a dish without dairy products. *Please!*" He pointed to the table again. "Make yourself comfortable."

The man didn't wait for Lilly to respond. He was probably used to picky Americans and had better things to do. Like tend to the other tables.

Lilly sat at the table and watched the people passing by on the street, waiting for the kind man to return. A couple walked by holding hands and she thought of Marco. Another couple stopped in front of the window and kissed. She thought of Marco again. Even when she ordered a glass of wine with her meal she thought of Marco.

It would take awhile to get over him, she was sure of it.

After the best pasta pomodoro she'd had in her entire life and two glasses of wine, she felt no urge for an emergency visit to the restroom. Lilly made her way toward the Trevi Fountain, which was just a few hundred feet away.

There were thousands of people taking pictures in front of the most famous fountain in the world while others tossed coins in the water for good luck. Lilly admired the tritons and the horses and the cascading water, her mind flashing back to a movie she saw a long time ago.

La Dolce Vita.

She had the urge to throw caution to the wind and wade

174

in the water like the actress in that movie, but getting arrested in Italy wasn't the greatest idea. Still, she had thought about it. Why did she have such an urge to be so spontaneous suddenly?

She knew why.

Marco.

The man got her to see life again. To experience it. To enjoy it.

She glanced over at the kiosk offering tours of Italy. A brochure caught her attention and curiosity drew her closer to the kiosk.

It was a brochure for boat tours of Faraglione di Mezzo.

Lilly smiled, thinking of her time with Marco on the boat. It didn't end so well with the jellyfish but the rest was wonderful. The water. The rocks. The kiss.

She turned the brochure over, admiring the beautiful photos and reading the description of Faraglione di Mezzo. Her heart rate picked up speed with every word.

"This can't be," she mumbled to herself, now wondering if she would pass out.

She read it again.

Faraglione di Mezzo is known to many as Temple of the Sea. It is considered good luck to kiss underneath the archway and many of those kisses have led to marriage proposals. That's why it is also affectionately known as the Temple of Groom.

She thought back to Madam Love again and her words at Panda Express.

There's a temple connected to the man Lilly will meet. Her future husband.

Lilly felt weak and took a seat on the bench.

What a fool.

She continued to people-watch, knowing soon she would return home to her plain-as-her-morning-bagel life. Her well-planned life.

Her life without Marco.

Marco stared at his computer screen in his hotel room in Rome and had great difficulty focusing on the task at hand. He tried again to work on a few things pertaining to his trip to Australia but just couldn't. He didn't have the energy. He didn't have the willpower.

All he had was an obsession for Lilly.

The woman he loved.

It was embarrassing how she dismissed him with nothing more than a handshake.

What the hell was that all about?

But his behavior was even more embarrassing than hers. He should have fought for her. He should have taken her in his arms right in front of Roberto and kissed the hell out of her.

Yes, it may have seemed crazy since he was leaving for Australia but they would have figured things out. Hell, he should have just told her he would quit his job to stop traveling. To be with her. Either that or he should have invited her to come with him to Australia.

"That wouldn't work," he mumbled to himself. "Stupid idea."

She had a job. People were counting on her and she wouldn't just bail on them and run off with Marco. It would have been nice though.

Still, she was so cold when they said goodbye. Like she was going back to her former self or like she had no feelings for him. Or maybe it was Roberto.

Yeah. That had to be it.

He shook his head and stood, walking over to the window for a stretch and a chance to clear his head. He stared out the window at the fountain below. There were over two thousand fountains in Rome, and even though the one he was looking at had to be one of the smallest, it was still beautiful. Not like the Trevi Fountain, but still. Beautiful.

"Wait a minute..." Marco paced back and forth in the hotel room. "That's right..."

Lilly would be at the Trevi Fountain before her flight.

He checked his watch. If she had to be at the airport two hours before her flight and it took thirty minutes to get to the airport, there was a good possibility she was there at the fountain at that moment. The more he thought about it, the more certain he was.

Marco closed his laptop, grabbed the room key and his wallet and ran out the door. He was going to see Lilly. He would profess his love and then they would figure things out. There had to be a way for it to work out.

Why didn't he think of this earlier? He could see her again at the Trevi Fountain!

He flagged down the first taxi outside of the hotel and hopped in. "La fontana di trevi. Per favore presto!"

"Nessun problema," said the driver, assuring Marco he would get him to the fountain fast.

Every block the taxi traveled, the faster Marco's heart raced.

Don't mess around this time. Say how you feel. Show her. Tell her you love her.

When the taxi arrived Marco paid the driver, thanked him, and got out in one motion. He wouldn't be surprised if the taxi had still been moving when he jumped out.

Ten seconds later Marco stood near the fountain, scanning the crowd. "This is insane." He couldn't believe how many people were there, at least a thousand. He moved through them with precision, weaving in and around like a NASCAR driver at the Indy 500. "Lilly!"

He was on a mission. Find the girl. Nothing else mattered.

"Lilly!" he yelled again, waiting for a response. Any response at all.

Nothing.

His eyes darted from the left to the right, searching. She had to be there somewhere. It was still early.

Two young Italian children ran around Marco. They laughed and chased each other back and forth, not a care in the world. They ended up back with their parents, doing circles around them, grabbing their legs. A happy family.

Marco wanted that. And why not with Lilly?

His gaze moved away from the kids and their parents to a woman a few feet away from them. She looked just like—

"Lilly!"

Marco ran toward her, bumping into several people, apologizing along the way.

Yes! Don't mess around. And don't take no for an answer. She loves you as much as you love her.

He grabbed her by the arm and swung her around, about to burst with happiness because he found her. "Lilly."

The woman pulled her arm free from Marco's grip. "Let go of me."

A man approached and got in Marco's face. "How dare you put your hand on my wife?"

"Sorry," said Marco. "I'm looking for someone. Sorry. Forgive me, please."

The man gave Marco a look and walked off with his wife.

Not only did Marco feel horrible that the woman wasn't Lilly but he wouldn't have blamed the man one bit if he had punched Marco in the face. Maybe Marco would have felt better if the man punched him. That might take his mind off Lilly.

No such luck.

Marco stood there, staring into the water in the fountain.

It was sinking in now.

Lilly was gone.

For good.

Chapter Eighteen

Lilly could barely keep her eyes open at work because of the jet lag. It was her first day back in the office after returning from Italy and it felt like someone was stabbing her eyeballs with needles. Low energy did not make for a productive workday and she had a lot to do. She took another big swig of coffee and tried to power through it.

Lilly glanced over at the file on her desk for Roberto. The job offer had about six hours left on it and she still hadn't heard from him. It didn't seem very promising considering the time. Odds were it wouldn't be a good day.

The day before hadn't been much fun either. Colette had stopped by the house and Lilly filled her in on everything over a bottle of wine. How she'd met Marco. Getting sick. Going viral in Italy. Missing the appointment with Roberto. Changing her hair color—which Colette loved. The jellyfish incident and visit to the emergency room. And the moronic treatment of Marco in the hotel when they'd said goodbye.

What a fool!

"I miss him," she said to herself, trying to fight back the tears. "I love him."

But seeing him again wouldn't happen thanks to her

unthinkable behavior.

The phone rang and just for a moment, Lilly had hoped it would be Marco. The number didn't show in her contacts, but he could have been calling from a different phone.

"Hello," she answered, crossing her fingers.

"Lilly, it's Roberto."

She sat up in her chair, suddenly not feeling any jet lag at all. "Hey! What a surprise."

Take the job.

"Is the offer still open?"

Lilly's pulse picked up speed. "Yes. Yes, it's still open. You changed your mind?"

"I did."

"Great!" Lilly screamed and threw her hands up in the air. She jumped up from her chair and picked up the desktop calendar she had just swatted to the floor. She set it back in its place and smiled. "Wonderful, wonderful. Janet will flip. In fact, everyone will flip. What made you change your mind?"

"Gabriella did, actually."

"Wow! So, she wanted to come to the US after all? Can't blame her…"

Roberto hesitated before answering. "Well, she said no to the proposal."

"Oh… I'm so sorry, Roberto."

Lilly wasn't expecting that. She was thrilled Roberto would join the company but didn't like the thought of anyone suffering from heartbreak. She knew what he was going through since her heart hurt too.

"What can a guy do?" Roberto said. "In all honesty, I rushed it and scared her off. She was fine the way things were. We'd only been dating for a few months but I fell head over heels for her. Now I just want to leave Italy, get as far away as possible, since everything here reminds me of her. So, my loss is your gain."

Sometimes you know the moment you meet a person you want to spend the rest of your life with them. There's something special about them. Something clicks between the two of you. Lilly had only spent a few days with Marco and she felt that way. He was fun to be around. Handsome. Smart. And he made her feel like she was the only woman in the world. She would have said yes to him.

"Maybe she wasn't the one after all and your true love awaits you in California," Lilly said, hoping that might make him feel better. "Things happen for a reason and you have to wait to find out what that reason is."

"Yeah…"

"I'm sorry for what happened but we're thrilled to have you back."

After Lilly said goodbye to Roberto, she called Janet's extension and gave her the news. She leaned back in her chair, certain the company would be okay. No more layoffs was a good thing. And she owed it all to Marco. She would have never been able to track Roberto down if it wasn't for his help.

Marco.

Just the thought of him drained her energy again. Another phone ring provided a much needed distraction. She eyed the caller ID. Colette.

Lilly closed her office door. "Hey!"

Colette laughed. "This is a surprise. You sound so upbeat."

"Don't get used to it. It's a temporary high because Roberto accepted the job offer."

"That's wonderful. Meet me for lunch and we'll celebrate."

"Stop it."

Colette was already back to trying to get Lilly to do something spontaneous. But it wasn't going to happen. Any spontaneity she felt had been left in Italy.

"Come on, Lilly."

"No. Nothing is so important that it can't be said over the phone."

"Not even if I want to tell you about a certain pregnancy?"

Lilly stared at the phone. This was the most beautiful news in the world ever. Colette and Simon were so happy together and this just made their relationship even more special.

A baby!

Lilly sniffled, trying to get a congratulations out of her

mouth. It wasn't coming out.

"Are you crying?" asked Colette.

Lilly sniffled again. "Of course I'm crying. I'm so happy for you and Simon."

"Okay, then. Well…crap. I feel guilty then because I'm not pregnant. It's my hair stylist, Jenny. You've met her, right?"

"Oh my God! I'm hanging up on you."

"No! Not while we're happy for Jenny!"

"I'm not happy for Jenny. I don't even *know* Jenny."

"Oh, stop it. Meet me for lunch. It's important."

"You know the routine, Colette."

"I know, I know. If we didn't plan it, you will ban it. This is different though."

"What is it? Honestly or I swear——"

"I can't say over the phone."

"Oh no you don't! I am *not* meeting you at Panda Express for lunch!"

"You have to."

Lilly huffed and paced back and forth in her office. She might try to find spontaneity in the future—or not—but today, no way. She wouldn't say anything to Colette but Lilly was going to Madam Love's office during her lunch to give that fraud a piece of her mind. It wasn't right getting people's hopes up like that and Madam Love needed to know how Lilly felt.

As for her best friend, Colette wasted no time at all. She

was back to her tricky ways. But Lilly wouldn't fall for it. And considering what had happened with her and Marco, plus Roberto's sad breakup, Lilly wasn't in the mood to do anything at all. That's why she'd decided she would skip the Elizabeth Gilbert event the next day. She wasn't up for it. Lilly was in the mood to throw herself a pity party. No balloons or cake necessary. Just a bowl of popcorn, a box of tissues and a few sad movies guaranteed to make her cry and she would be set.

"Lilly? Talk to me. Meet me for lunch."

"No. And I won't be able to attend Elizabeth Gilbert's event tomorrow night either."

"What?" screamed Colette. "Don't you dare! It's sold out and we have been planning it forever."

"I'm just not in the mood."

"So we're back to that again? Who spent ten hours helping you move into your new place last year?"

Let the guilt trip begin. "You."

"And who let you borrow her car for two days when your car was having work done on it?"

"You" Lilly waited for one more example. Colette always did things in threes.

"And who loves you more than anyone?"

"Maybe you. Although sometimes I have my doubts. Look, take your mom to Elizabeth Gilbert."

"No. You owe me this. You know how much I have wanted to go to this and I want her to sign my book! Don't you dare cancel."

"I have to get back to work, Colette. I'll talk with you later."

She ended the call with Colette and stuffed the phone into her purse. She took the elevator down to the first floor and headed for the parking lot.

Ten minutes later Lilly parked her Toyota Corolla in the farthest spot of the strip mall, hoping to avoid door dings or any other disasters.

Lilly passed the yoga place and Noah's Bagels, swinging the front door open to Madam Love's office. The lobby and front desk were empty but a few seconds later, Madam Love passed through the hanging beads and smiled. She was dressed in bright red blouse, her long hair held together under a headband. "I've been expecting you, darling."

Lilly placed her hands on her hips, her only mission to wipe that smile off her face. "Don't *darling* me. The only reason you knew I would come looking for you is because you knew I would catch on to your lies. How do you sleep at night?"

"On my side with a full-length body pillow. I snore less that way."

"You know what I mean!"

"Hey, don't take it out on me. You're the one that likes to sabotage your own life. But hey, if you want to talk about what happened, no problem. Fifty dollars. Will that be cash or charge?"

Rich Amooi

Lilly blinked. "You seriously want me to pay you money after what you did?"

"I should charge you double for not taking my advice."

"Not taking your…" She couldn't believe she was having this conversation with Madam Love. As if *Lilly* was in the wrong here? "What advice did I *not* take?"

"I told you not to mess with nature."

"I didn't mess with nature."

"Oh yes you did."

"How?"

Madam Love held out her hand and snapped her fingers. "Fifty dollars and I'll tell you what you did wrong. I'll also tell you how you can fix it."

"It can't be fixed."

"Not with *that* attitude, it can't."

Did Lilly really mess with nature? Maybe she did for not telling Marco how she felt and for the way she said goodbye. She thought there was a possibility

"Lilly," said Madam Love, tapping her fingers on reception counter. "Answer the question. That's the only way I can help you. Did you mess with nature? Yes or no?"

"It's a small possibility," she mumbled.

Madam Love leaned closer. "What was that?"

"It doesn't matter if I did or not. I screwed up. It's over."

"That's where you're wrong. It's *not* over. Fifty bucks or you can be sad for the rest of your life."

Lilly stared at Madam Love's outstretched hand. Why

was she even considering it now? Maybe because she didn't want to give up on Marco, that's why.

Lilly opened her purse and pulled out a credit card, sliding it across the counter. "I can't believe I'm doing this."

Madam Love winked. "I knew you would."

"Oh!" Lilly lunged for the credit card but couldn't reach it.

Madam Love quickly swiped the card through the machine, smiled, and handed it back to Lilly "I'm just having fun with you. You need to loosen up." She handed Lilly the receipt and slid a pen her way. "By the way, I prefer tips in cash, but Uncle Sam doesn't need to know that."

Lilly huffed and signed the receipt, leaving it on the counter with the pen. "You expect a tip too? Wow, you've got some serious hutzpah."

"Thank you for noticing." Madam Love pulled back the bead curtain and waved Lilly through. "Straight back through the open door. Your future awaits you."

Lilly ducked under the beads and walked into the room, looking around. It was cozy, dim, except for the light from the numerous battery-powered candles. Everything was red and purple: the curtains, the furniture, even the floor rug.

Across from Madam Love's chair was a comfy loveseat with over-sized cushions. On the table between the chair and loveseat sat a crystal ball so big she could drill three holes and go bowling with it.

Lilly pointed to the crystal ball. "When we met you told

me you didn't use these things. Too *old school* for you, I think were your exact words."

Madam Love nodded. "Some clients insist on the crystal ball and nothing else. I never use it for house calls or Panda Express calls since it's a bitch to carry around. Okay, let's get down to business. Take a deep breath and then tell me where it all went wrong."

Lilly hesitated and then took a deep breath. "*You* were wrong. Your prediction. What do you have to say about that?"

Madam Love rubbed the crystal ball. "Just to let you know, I'm not rubbing the ball for answers. I just love the way it feels. Smooth. Do you want to touch it?"

"No."

She removed her hands from the ball and rubbed them together. "Okay then. Regarding your accusation of me being wrong…*you're* the one who's wrong."

"First, the bear you told me I would see wasn't a bear at all. Well, yes, it was a bear *mascot*. But not a real bear."

"I don't recall telling you you'd see a *real* bear. I'm sure my exact words were you would see a bear. Did you or did you not see a bear? Real or otherwise?"

"I did, but—"

"No buts. What else do you have an issue with?"

"What about the expensive car you said I would ride in? It belonged to my boss, so it didn't count."

"Why doesn't that count?"

Lilly thought for a moment. She didn't have a good answer for her. "I don't know. It just doesn't count. Okay, forget about that stuff. You told me I would meet my future husband if I left the country."

"You did."

Lilly made the sound of a buzzer. "Wrong!" She held up her ring finger. "Do I look engaged to you? Or married? I think not."

"I told you that you would meet him. I didn't say you would come home engaged or married."

"I didn't meet *the one* obviously."

"Yes, you did."

"Who is it then? Marco? Roberto?"

"I don't know his name."

"Not a surprise."

Madam Love leaned forward in her chair. "Lilly, let me ask you this. Do you want to get married or not? And this is another yes or no question."

Lilly took another deep breath. "Yes."

"Good! Then be open to it. I didn't say you would be married right away. Being open to it, without obsessing over it, sets the wheels in motion."

"I *was* open to it."

"*Was* isn't acceptable. Be open to it *now*. Always. How does the universe know what you want if you keep sending Her mixed signals?"

"Well…"

"Knock it off."

Lilly folded her arms. "You don't have to be mean about it."

Madam Love pointed to Lilly. "I'm not being mean. I'm being firm. Unfold your arms."

Lilly hesitated and then unfolded her arms.

"Good. Now listen up. You have to be open...physically and mentally. Keep those shoulders up and the head held high. Confidence. Don't go hide in the corner. Get out. Have fun. And soon you will see the miracle of life. The miracle of love."

Like it was that easy.

Lilly sat up, her brain trying to assimilate what Madam Love had just said. It sounded reasonable—mostly—but her heart was on a mission to reject every single word.

Lilly sighed. "I don't know what to think anymore."

"It's hard for your head to stay clear when it's being bombarded by pollution. I'm just trying to keep you on course. Read my lips. This isn't over yet. Do not alter any plans you have this week."

On the way back to work she called Colette to let her know they were back on for Elizabeth Gilbert the next night. That wouldn't be a nice thing to do, anyway—bail on her at the last moment. And Lilly would try to follow Madam Love's advice and be open and strong.

She knew it wouldn't be easy.

Chapter Nineteen

Lilly and Colette stood from their seats with the other attendees at the Greek Theater in Berkeley and gave Elizabeth Gilbert a standing ovation. Elizabeth talked for over an hour and a half about women, obstacles, fear, her writing career, and her love life.

Elizabeth did exactly what Lilly's father and last boyfriend did—she'd left everything behind to go find herself.

Colette hugged Lilly. "That was amazing. What did you think?"

Lilly crinkled her nose. "She talked about Italy a lot. And that was a weird coincidence when she talked about the time she spoke at the All About Women Festival in Australia."

"What's so weird about it?"

Lilly shrugged. "Marco is in Australia."

Colette laughed and rubbed Lilly's back. "You're still high on Marco, I get it. I think if you try hard enough, you'll be able to connect anything to him. Italian food. Wine. Kisses. Using the Pope as toilet paper."

Lilly pinched Colette's arm when her best friend laughed. "Not funny."

Colette perked up. "Maybe you need to fly to Australia

193

and go get that man."

"Not even… Okay, let's get moving so we can beat some of the crowd out of the parking lot."

"Hold on!" Colette pulled a book by Elizabeth Gilbert from her purse and showed Lilly. "We still need to get in line for the book signing. I want her to sign this and get a picture with her."

Lilly sighed. "You already have a signed book from her."

"That was a different book. Let's go."

"No way. That could take an hour or two waiting in line for that. I'm tired and I want to go home and read in bed." *Or cry in bed, more likely.*

Colette shook her head. "You owe me."

"I owe *you*?"

"Yes. Who was the one who cooked soup for you every single day when you had the flu last winter?"

"I'm not playing this guilt game anymore. Let's go home."

<<<>>>

Marco scanned the crowd at the Greek Theater and shook his head, panicking. Elizabeth Gilbert had just left the stage and was on her way to sign books for her fans. He'd never seen so many women in one place before and he needed to find Lilly.

He considered himself lucky that he could find a ticket

to the sold-out event on Craigslist. The seller should have felt guilty selling him a ticket in the last row for three times the original cost, but the guy just smiled as he took Marco's money and asked him if he also wanted tickets to see Paul Simon. No thanks. The only thing he wanted at that moment was Lilly.

Marco had to admit that Elizabeth Gilbert was an engaging speaker, even though he only paid attention one third of the time. Most of the evening he scanned the thousands of women at the outdoor theater, looking for Lilly. The problem was he could only see the backs of their heads since he sat all the way in the back.

A few times he tried to sneak up to the front or pretended he was looking for the bathroom in the lower section. He wasn't sneaky enough, though, and was caught each time by security and told to return to his seat. It would have been much easier if he knew where she worked instead of showing up at an event with thousands of people.

Why didn't he ever ask where she worked? He had Lilly's phone number, but this was something that had to be done in person.

Marco needed to get the truth. He needed to know if she loved him. If they had a future together. If she said she didn't love him, so be it. He would let her go, never bother her again.

Time was running out, and he needed a new plan. If he didn't act fast, she would slip away and all would be lost. He had two options. Run outside to the street, hoping he would spot her there. Or go to the book signing and find her there.

Which one?

"Choose one, don't stand here and waste time," he said to himself.

"Excuse me?" said the woman he bumped into.

"Nothing. Sorry."

Book signing. Go.

He jumped over the seats in front of him and sprinted down the row to the aisle. He weaved in and out of the countless women, closer to the signing area down by the stage. The line was long, hundreds of women, but again their backs were to Marco. Too bad the area was roped off and the only thing he could do was stand in line. Then maybe he could ask the women one by one if he could cut ahead of them so he could go profess his love to the most beautiful woman in the world.

Marco's plan was cut short when he was stopped by security again. "Sorry, sir. This line is for the book signing only."

He looked over the security guards shoulder down the long line. "No problem. I'd like a book signed."

The security guard eyed Marco from head to toe. "Where's the book?"

Oh.

Marco hadn't thought of that.

He glanced at the women in line, all of them already

holding books to be signed. "I can't buy the books when I get up to the front?"

The security guard shook his head. "You need to have the item in your hands before you get in line."

Crap. That's not what I wanted to hear. "Where do I buy the books?"

The security guard swung around and pointed to the upper level of the outdoor theater. "Up there. On either side you'll find plenty of books and other items for purchase. But you better hurry, they may already be sold out and we don't know how long Ms. Gilbert will be signing."

"Thanks for letting me know."

Marco jumped over another set of chairs and ran as fast as he could to the upper level. He entered the giant tent filled with tables and displays of books, t-shirts, hats, beach towels, pins, you name it.

Marco grabbed a book and dropped a twenty-dollar bill on the table for the employee, not waiting for the change. Less than two minutes later he approached the same security guard and held up the book for him to see.

The security guard smiled. "You don't waste time."

Marco was out of breath but he returned the smile. "Life is too short for wasting time."

The security guard gestured for Marco to pass through.

Marco turned to look behind him and the security guard was already talking to someone else. Now was the time for him to make his move. Standing in line would do him no good.

He passed the women in the line, moving as quickly as he could, excusing himself, careful to check every face.

Where was she? She had to be there.

"Lilly!" Marco yelled, moving closer to Elizabeth Gilbert. "Lilly!"

"I can be your Lilly!" said a woman.

Her statement was followed by laughter from many of the other women, but Marco didn't respond. He moved forward, weaving in and out of a few more women until he saw the front. Under the bright light, Elizabeth Gilbert sat at a table, head down signing a book. She looked up and smiled for a picture, then greeted the next person in line.

Lilly.

Marco's heart raced as he watched her next to another woman who must have been her best friend Colette. Marco stared at Lilly, now feeling everything would be all right. He would tell her how he felt, then ask her if she felt the same. After that he would find out what she was doing for the rest of her life.

He took a step in her direction and was grabbed by the arm. It was the same security guard from earlier and this time he wasn't smiling. "I'm going to ask you to leave. Cutting in line is prohibited."

Marco let out a desperate breath of frustration. "It's not what you think. I need to talk to that woman who's at the table right now. Not Elizabeth Gilbert. The fan. I'm just trying to get up there before she leaves."

"And *I'm* just doing my job. I can't allow you to proceed forward. We have protocol for these events and it's not fair to the people in line if people break the rules. Please come with me."

The security guard continued to hold Marco's arm.

"I just want to know if she loves me, that's all." Marco heard several audible *ahhhs* from the women around him but he maintained eye contact with the man. "I want to talk with the girl. I'm in love with her. Please. I promise I'm not going to get the book signed. "

"That's just it. I need to enforce the rules. This area is for book signings only. I can lose my job if I let you break the rules. I have a wife and kid to provide for."

Marco nodded. "I understand."

"Why don't you go wait by the book signing exit," a woman piped in. "Get her when she leaves."

This was the beauty of a woman's brain. They analyzed things differently. Why hadn't he thought of that?

He turned and smiled at the woman. "Great idea. Thank you." He turned and eyed Elizabeth Gilbert's table and Lilly was no longer there. "She's gone! Somebody please point me in the right direction. The book signing exit, please!"

The security guard released Marco's arm and slapped him on the back. "Follow me."

<<<>>>

Lilly exited the book signing, passed through the gate, and headed out toward the street. Colette was on top of the world, opening her book and staring at Elizabeth Gilbert's autograph. She held the book toward Lilly as they walked, showing off what the author had written. "She would die to have my hair. Can you believe that? Elizabeth Gilbert wants to have my hair."

Lilly could. Just about everyone she encountered wanted to have Colette's long blonde hair. In the past Lilly would have wanted it too, but she was happy with her new do she got in Italy.

In Italy with Marco.

There she went again, not even able to go a few minutes without thinking of *him*.

They walked down Hearst Avenue to the parking lot. Soon she would be home in bed, most likely dreaming of the man who stole her heart. That wasn't helping her any, and she needed to forget about him but easier said than done. She blew it and that was that.

Lilly took another step and then stopped, spotting a familiar looking man waving to her from across the street. He looked like—

"What?" said Colette. "Are you okay?" Colette followed Lilly's gaze to the other side of the street. "And *who* is the hunky man coming toward us? He seems to know you."

Lilly couldn't get a word out. She stared as Marco came closer.

He wasn't in Australia. He was in Berkeley, California.

If she had the strength she would ask Colette to call an ambulance. Lilly was going to pass out any second. She felt her eyes burn and needed to cut off the tears before they happened. She didn't understand why he was there or how he found her but it was still so good to see him.

Marco stopped in front of her and jammed his hands in his pockets. "Lilly."

"Marco… What are you doing here?"

"I think you know why I'm here."

Lilly studied him for a minute and let a tiny smile form on her mouth. "You're an Elizabeth Gilbert fan?"

Marco's gaze penetrated her. "I'm a Lilly Jones fan."

Colette sighed. "Oh my. I love where this is going." She pointed over to the planter in front of the parking lot. "I'm just going to sit right over there. Just pretend I'm not here even though I'll be listening to every single word. Take your time."

"I don't get it," said Lilly, trying to comprehend how Marco found her and why he wanted to find her. He was supposed to be in Australia.

Marco took another step toward her. "Lilly Pilly."

"Marco Polo."

He grinned, and that was almost enough to send Lilly into cardiac arrest. She missed that smile.

She missed him.

Loved him.

Marco took another step and now they were inches apart. "I'm curious—"

"First, let me tell you I'm sorry for what I did in Sorrento at the hotel, the way I treated you. The way I said goodbye. It was wrong and I regret it and I—"

He pushed his index finger against her lips. "Shhhh. Let's not talk about the past. Really. I came here to ask you a question. Just one question."

"Okay. I'm ready."

He grabbed both of her hands and massaged the tops of them with his thumbs. "Look me in the eyes and don't look anywhere else until you answer the question. Got it?"

Her heart was going to explode. "Got it."

"Do you love me?"

Colette sighed. "Oh, this is the sweetest. I should be videotaping it."

Lilly wanted to melt right there. Her eyes burned even more and this time she couldn't stop the tears flowing down her face. She couldn't stop the emotions either and why should she?

Like Madam Love said, she shouldn't mess with nature. She wanted to kiss him all night long. Heck, there were plenty of other things she wanted to do to him. But most importantly, she wanted to be with him. And she wanted to tell him how much she loved him. But it felt like there was a golf ball in her throat and she couldn't get the words out.

Marco rubbed the tops of Lilly's hands again with his thumbs. "I'm getting worried, Lilly. You're not answering."

"Quit worrying the man," said Colette, loud enough for the entire neighborhood to hear. "Answer the damn question."

"I love you, Marco."

Marco moved his hands to her hips, pulling her closer until their bodies touched. "That's exactly what I wanted to hear. I love you too."

Then he kissed her.

On the sidewalk in Berkeley.

Thousands of miles away from Australia.

And everything was good.

No.

Everything was perfect.

Lilly pulled away from the kiss, curiosity getting the best of her. "What about Australia? What happened?"

"I never went since I'm quitting my job. That was no way to live and how could I see my girlfriend Lilly if I was on the road all the time?"

"Girlfriend…" said Lilly, loving the way it sounded.

"Yes!" screamed Colette, jumping up from the planter. "Lilly's got a boyfriend!"

Lilly shook her head and laughed, gesturing to her best friend. "Marco, meet Colette. Colette, this is Marco." She smiled. "My boyfriend."

Chapter Twenty

Eight months later.

Madam Love's eyes grew wide. So did her smile. She leaned in to Marco and Lilly and whispered. "I see triplets in your future."

Lilly blinked. "That's not funny."

She wanted to have kids. Maybe even two or three. Not at the same time!

Marco furled his eyebrows. "If you upset Lilly you will not be getting a tip."

Madam Love frowned. "Hey, hey. Come on—loosen up. By the way, I can't remember if I told you but cash tips are always preferred." She winked. "But Uncle Sam doesn't need to know about that."

"You mentioned that. Twice. Can we get on with this?"

"Of course, of course, darling."

Lilly glanced across the San Francisco Bay toward Alcatraz and smiled, shaking her head. Having her wedding on a Hornblower yacht wasn't her original plan. The mansion on the peninsula they had secured for the big day had burned down just yesterday, so they had to improvise.

Instead of stressing out over the two months of planning for that venue flushed down the toilet, she took a deep breath and went in a different direction. Marco had suggested taking one of the most memorable events from Italy and incorporating that into the wedding. She'd thought of the boat ride out to the Faraglioni rocks and that kiss. That's how they came up with the wedding on the water, floating near Alcatraz—also known as "The Rock."

Nothing could ruin this day.

Madam Love pressed the button on her iPad and scrolled a little, searching. She looked up and smiled again. "Dearly beloved, we are gathered here today to celebrate the love of Lilly and Marco…who may or may not be having triplets soon."

Marco cleared his throat.

"Right. Anyway, this morning I took a few moments to search Webster's Dictionary for the word *love*. My first thought was…who is Webster and how did he get a dictionary?"

The guests laughed and Lilly let it go. Madam Love was improvising.

"My second thought was…can you define love so easily? I don't think you can. In fact, there are plenty of other four-letter words that are much easier to define. But we need not get into those right now. Come find me during the cocktail hour if you'd like to discuss them." She winked and continued. "Marco and Lilly have written their own vows and will read them now."

Marco pulled a piece of paper from his jacket pocket and unfolded it. He gazed up at Lilly, grinning that grin that always sent a tickle from her throat to her stomach, then back up to her heart.

"Lilly. My love. This is the best day of my life because I'm marrying the girl who makes my heart sing. A little off key maybe, but still *sing* nonetheless. There's no doubt in my mind we were made for each other. They say relationships go through their ups and downs, which is great considering we've already had most of our downs. That means the future will be bright, beautiful, exciting. Thank you for making me the happiest man in the world." He smiled, folded the piece of paper and stuck it back in his jacket pocket. "Oh, and thanks in advance for the triplets."

Lilly smirked. "I love you but triplets are *not* happening."

Madam Love let out an evil laugh. "We'll see about that now, won't we?"

Colette reached over to hand Lilly the three-by-five cards that had her vows but Lilly waved her off. "I don't need those. I will try to be spontaneous here."

Marco grinned. "That's my girl."

Lilly smiled and took a deep breath. "Marco. My love. I have been to hell and back with you."

The guests laughed and Marco shrugged. "This is true."

"And I would do it all again in a heartbeat. Thank you for making me the happiest woman in the world." She eyed his lips. "Can we kiss now?"

Marco perked up. "Sounds good."

Madam Love's hand came up and kept them separated. "Not yet. You two keep it in your pants."

"Hurry," Lilly said.

"Yeah," Marco added. "Hurry."

Not long after that Lilly and Marco were married and kissed.

Since the reservation for the yacht was last minute, they couldn't get a private room on the yacht and shared the buffet line with eight hundred other people: tourists, locals, other couples in love. And Lilly wouldn't have changed it for the world. Because when it came down to it, it wasn't about the place or the food or the how many flowers were in each centerpiece. It was about love. It was about being together. They could have gotten married anywhere and she would still have had that same special feeling in her heart.

Marco kissed Lilly again and smiled. He couldn't believe that just a little over eight months ago he was single, not even thinking about relationships.

His life had transformed in less than a year. Marco had quit his job and gone into business with his best friend. Stefano had stock options in his startup company and cashed out after it went public. He put up all the money to get started and they were now winemakers. And since Lilly worked in sales and marketing before she went into human resources, the plan was for her to join the company in six months. Everything was falling into place and life couldn't be better.

After the buffet meal, Marco held out his hand to Lilly. "Join me on the deck for a few minutes?"

Lilly took his hand and stood. "Of course."

They made their way to the top deck of the yacht and walked toward the back. Marco smiled and pulled her close. "Hello Mrs. Santini."

"Hello Mr. Santini."

Marco pointed toward Angel Island as the Hornblower yacht got closer. "Did you know it's good luck to kiss here?"

Lilly stared out at Angel Island and smiled. "Is that right?"

Marco nodded. "*Very* good luck."

Lilly bent forward to look over the rail down to the water. "I don't want to fall over and repeat what happened with the jellyfish."

"I don't think there's a chance of that. First, the water is much colder here than in Italy, so you would die of hypothermia or get eaten by a great white shark long before the jellyfish did any serious damage."

"That's comforting to know." Lilly reached for the rail and tried to shake it. "Seems sturdy."

Marco grabbed the rail and squeezed it. "I think you're

safe. Ready?"

"Yes."

He leaned forward and kissed Lilly, pulling her closer.

"Lilly! Marco!" Madam Love rushed toward them, a desperate look on her face. "I know you were in the middle of a little smoochy smoochy but I had to find you and tell you I was wrong about my prediction. You're not going to have triplets."

Marco chuckled. "It's okay. We were skeptical, so don't worry about it. I'm sure a psychic can have an off day and —"

"You're going to have quadruplets!"

THE END
<<<<>>>>

Acknowledgements

Dear Reader,

I truly hope you enjoyed Marco and Lilly's story. I must say, I had fun torturing Lilly. LOL. I know, I'm bad, but I still gave her a happy-ever-after!

I would like to give a HUGE shout-out to my fans around the world. Thank you! It means the world to me that you read my books, and it still blows me away I can do this for a living. Thank you for all the wonderful reviews on Amazon and Goodreads! Your letters and messages motivate me and help me write faster, so keep them coming. Please send me an email to say hello. I personally reply to everyone. My email address is rich@richamooi.com.

So many people helped to make this book possible, and I'd like to take a moment to say thank you and acknowledge them here.

Thanks to the amazing Sue Traynor for drawing the perfect book cover for this story. You're the best!

To Mary Yakovets. Editing is a crucial part of the publishing process and I thank you for making me look better.

It would have been impossible to write and publish this book without help from Michael Hauge, Cathy Yardley, Becky Monson, Deb Julienne, Whitney Dineen, Christina Britton, Julie Carver, Hannah Jayne, Debbie Mekler, Romance Writers of America, Silicon Valley RWA, Indie Author Collective, Chick Lit Chat, and the top-secret Facebook Group, AC. Thank you for your feedback and support.

Special thanks to my alpha reader and hot Spanish wife, Silvi Martin, who gives me the best feedback. She also writes contemporary romance.
Find her here: http://www.silvimartin.com.

My beta readers help me improve the story and I'm forever grateful for their awesome feedback. A big thanks going out to Maché, Isabel, Robert, Deb, Julita, and Krasimir.

Until next time… Be happy. Be grateful.

Made in the USA
Middletown, DE
09 June 2016